MISTR

Deth laughed, hi   So.
You think, in th   ing
matters?"

"It matters! I have inherited a shape-changer's power.
Look . . ." Something—the wine, his indifference, her
hopelessness—made Raederle reckless. She stretched out
her hand, held it curved in a motionless caress to the
heat and curve of a flame.

Deep within her, rousing out of a dormant, lawless
heritage, wordless knowledge of fire filled her. She
touched the flame, then let it lie in her hand like a
flower.

"Look," she said, and closed her hand over it. The
night fell around her again as the tiny flame died. She
saw Deth's face, motionless, unreadable. His lips parted.

"Another riddle," he whispered. "Mathom trained
you well to be a riddle-master's wife."

"Topflight fantasy!"
—*ALA Booklist*

"Patricia McKillip has created a world populated by
mysterious harpists, riddle-masters who preserve the ancient
wisdoms in gaelic triad-like question/strictures, land-heirs
magically tied to their native soil, and overseeing it all, an
intriguing entity known only as the High One, who may be
many things. I couldn't put it down."

—Katherine Kurtz,
Author of *The
Chronicles of the
Deryni*

Heir of
Sea and Fire

Patricia A. McKillip

A Del Rey Book

BALLANTINE BOOKS • NEW YORK

A Del Rey Book
Published by Ballantine Books

Library of Congress Catalog Card Number: 77-4650

ISBN 0-345-27468-7

This edition published by arrangement with Atheneum

Manufactured in the United States of America

First Ballantine Books Edition: November 1978

Cover art and frontispiece by Darrell Sweet

MAP BY KATHY MCKILLIP

Notes on people and places may be found beginning on page 209.

1

IN SPRING, THREE THINGS CAME INVARIABLY TO
the house of the King of An: the year's first
shipment of Herun wine, the lords of the Three
Portions for the spring council, and an argument.
The spring of the year following the strange dis-
appearance of the Prince of Hed, who had, with the
High One's harpist, vanished like a mist in Isig
Pass, the great house with its seven gates and seven
white towers seemed to be cracking like a seed pod
out of a long, bitter winter of silence and grief. The
season dusted the air with green, set patterns of
light like inlay on the cold stone floors, and roused
restlessness like sap in the deep heart of An, until
Raederle of An, standing in Cyone's garden, which
no one had entered for the six months since her
death, felt that even the dead of An, their bones
plaited with grass root, must be drumming their
fingers in their graves.
    She stirred after a while, left the tangle of weeds
and withered things that had not survived the winter, and went back into the King's hall, whose doors
were flung wide to the light. Servants under the eye
of Mathom's steward, were shaking the folds out of

1

the lords' banners, hanging them precariously from the high beams. The lords were due any day, and the house was in a turmoil preparing to receive them. Already their gifts had been arriving for her: a milk-white falcon bred in the wild peaks of Osterland from the Lord of Hel; a brooch like a gold wafer from Map Hwillion, who was too poor to afford such things; a flute of polished wood inlaid with silver, which bore no name, and worried Raederle, since whoever had sent it had known what she would love. She watched the banner of Hel unrolling, the ancient boar's head with tusks like black moons on an oak-green field; it rose jerkily on its hangings to survey the broad hall out of its small fiery eyes. She gazed back at it, her arms folded, then turned suddenly and went to find her father.

She found him in his chambers arguing with his land-heir. Their voices were low, and they stopped when she entered, but she saw the faint flush on Duac's cheekbones. In the pale slashes of his brows and his sea-colored eyes, he bore the stamp of Ylon's wild blood, but his patience with Mathom when everyone else had exhausted theirs was considered phenomenal. She wondered what Mathom had said to upset him.

The King turned a dour crow's eye to her; she said politely, for his mood in the mornings was unpredictable, "I would like to visit Mara Croeg in Aum for a couple of weeks, with your permission. I could pack and leave tomorrow. I've been in Anuin all winter, and I feel—I need to get away."

There was not a flicker of change in his eyes. He said simply, "No," and turned to pick up his wine cup.

She stared at his back, annoyed, and discarded courtesy like an old shoe. "Well, I'm not going to stay here and be argued over like a prize cow out

2

of Aum. Do you know who sent me a gift? Map Hwillion. Only yesterday he was laughing at me for falling out of a pear tree, and now he's got his first beard and an eight-hundred-year-old house with a leaky roof, and he thinks he wants to marry me. You're the one who promised me to the Prince of Hed; can't you put a stop to all this? I'd rather listen to the pig herds of Hel during a thunderstorm than another spring council arguing with you about what to do with me."

"So would I," Duac murmured. Mathom eyed them both. His hair had turned iron-grey seemingly over night; his sorrow over Cyone's death had limned his face to the bone, but it had neither tempered nor bittered his disposition.

"What do you want me to tell them," he asked, "other than what I have told them for nineteen years? I have made a vow, binding beyond life, to marry you to the man winning Peven's game. If you want to run away and live with Map Hwillion under his leaky roof, I can't stop you—they know that."

"I don't want to marry Map Hwillion," she said, exasperated. "I would like to marry the Prince of Hed. Except that I don't know any more who he is, and no one else knows where he is. I am tired of waiting; I am tired of this house; I am tired of listening to the Lord of Hel tell me that I am being ignored and insulted by the Prince of Hed; I want to visit Mara Croeg in Aum, and I don't understand how you can refuse such a simple, reasonable request."

There was a short silence, during which Mathom considered the wine in his cup. An indefinable expression came into his face; he set the cup down and said, "If you like, you can go to Caithnard."

Her lips parted in surprise. "I can? To visit Rood? Is there a ship—" And then Duac brought his hand down flat on the wine table, rattling cups. "No."

She stared at him, astonished, and he closed his hand. His eyes were narrowed slightly as he gazed back at Mathom. "He's asked me to go, but I've already refused. He wants Rood home."

"Rood? I don't understand."

Mathom moved away from the window suddenly with an irritated whirl of sleeve. "I might as well have the entire council in here babbling at me at once. I want Rood to take a leave from his studies, come back to Anuin for a while; he'll take that fact best from either Duac or you."

"You tell him," Duac said inflexibly. Under the King's eye he yielded, sat down, gripping the arms of his chair as though he were holding fast to his patience. "Then will you explain so I can understand? Rood has just taken the Red of Apprenticeship; if he stays he'll take the Black at a younger age than any living Master. He's done fine work there; he deserves the chance to stay."

"There are more riddles in the world than those in the locked books behind the walls of that College in Caithnard."

"Yes. I've never studied riddle-mastery, but I have an idea that you can't answer them all at once. He's doing the best he can. What do you want him to do? Go lose himself at Erlenstar Mountain like the Prince of Hed?"

"No. I want him here."

"For what, in Hel's name? Are you planning to die or something?"

"Duac," Raederle breathed, but he waited stubbornly for the King to answer. She felt, like a live thing beneath the irritation and obstinacy in them both, the binding between them beyond all definition. Then Duac heaved himself to his feet at Mathom's silence and snapped before he slammed

4

the door behind him so hard the stones seemed to rattle, "By Madir's bones, I wish I could see into that peatbog you call a mind!"

Raederle sighed. She looked at Mathom, who seemed in spite of the rich robe he wore, black and impervious as a wizard's curse in the sunlight. "I'm beginning to hate spring. I won't ask you to explain the world to me, just why I can't go visit Mara Croeg while Cyn Croeg is here at the council."

"Who was Thanet Ross and why did he play a harp without strings?"

She stood a moment, dredging the answer out of interminable, half-forgotten hours of riddlery. Then she turned; she heard his voice again, just before the door slammed once more, "And stay out of Hel."

She found Duac in the library, staring out the window. She joined him, leaning against the window, looking down at the city that sloped gently away from the King's house to spill around the rim of the harbor. Trade-ships were drifting in with the midmorning tide, their colored sails deflating in the wind like weary sighs. She saw the white and green of Danan Isig's ships bringing the marvellous crafts from Isig Mountain; and a hope stirred in her that the northern Kingdom had sent news more valuable than all its beautiful cargo. Duac stirred beside her, as the peace of the ancient library with its smell of hide, wax and the iron of old shields returned the composure to his face. He said softly, "He is the most pig-headed, arbitrary and exasperating man in the Three Portions of An."

"I know."

"Something's going on in his head; something's bubbling behind his eyes like a bad spell . . . It worries me. Because if it came to a choice between a blind step into a bottomless pit with him and a walk across the apple orchards with the Lords of

An at their finest, I would shut my eyes and step. But what is he thinking?"

"I don't know." She dropped her chin in her palms. "I don't know why he wants us all home now. I don't understand him. I asked him why I couldn't leave, and he asked me why Thanet Ross played a harp with no strings."

"Who?" Duac looked at her. "How could . . . Why did he play a harp with no strings?"

"For the same reason he walked backward and shaved his head instead of his beard. For no reason except that there was no reason. He was a sad man and died backward."

"Oh."

"He was walking backward for no reason and fell in a river. Nobody ever saw him again, but they assumed he died since there was no reason—"

"All right," Duac protested mildly. "You could spin that one into yarn."

She smiled. "See what education you missed, not being destined to marry a riddle-master." Then her smile faded; she bowed her head, traced a crack in the old mortar. "I feel as though I'm waiting for a legend to come down from the north, breaking out of winter with the spring water . . . Then I remember the farmer's son who used to put shells to my ears so I could hear the sea, and, Duac, that's when I become afraid for him. He has been gone so long; there has not been one word from him for a year, and no one in the realm has heard so much as a harp-note from the High One's harpist. Surely the High One would never keep Morgon so long from his land. I think something must have happened to them in Isig Pass."

"As far as anyone knows, the land-rule hasn't passed from Morgon," Duac said comfortingly, but she only shifted restlessly.

"Then where is he? At least he could get a message to his own land. The traders say that every time they stop at Tol, Tristan and Eliard are there at the dock waiting, hoping for news. Even at Isig, with all they say happened to him, he managed to write. They say he has scars on his hands like vesta-horns, and he can take the shape of trees . . ."

Duac glanced down at his own hands as if he expected to see the withered moons of white horns in them. "I know . . . The simplest thing to do would be to go to Erlenstar Mountain and ask the High One where he is. It's spring; the Pass should be clearing. Eliard might do it."

"Leave Hed? He's Morgon's land-heir; they'd never let him leave."

"Maybe. But they say there's a streak of stubbornness long as a witch's nose in the people of Hed. He might." He leaned over the ledge suddenly; his head turned towards a distant, double-column of riders making their way across the meadows. "Here they come. In full plumage."

"Who is it?"

"I can't . . . blue. Blue and black retinue; that would be Cyn Croeg. He appears to have met someone green . . ."

"Hel."

"No. Green and cream; very small following."

She sighed. "Map Hwillion."

She stood by the window after Duac left to tell Mathom, watching the riders veer around the nut orchards, flickering in and out of the lacework of black, bare branches. They appeared again at a corner of the old city wall, to take the main road through the city, which led twisting and curving through the market and old high houses and shops whose windows would be wide open like eyes, full of watchers. By the time they disappeared through the gates of the city, she had decided what to do.

THREE DAYS LATER, SHE SAT BESIDE THE PIG-
woman of the Lord of Hel under an oak tree,
weaving grass blades into a net. From all around
her in the placid afternoon came the vast snort
and grumble of the great pig herds of Hel as
they stirred through the tangled roots and shadows
of oak. The pig-woman, whom no one had ever
bothered to name, was smoking a meditative pipe.
She was a tall, bony, nervous woman, with long,
dishevelled grey hair and dark grey eyes; she had
tended the pigs as long as anyone could remember.
They were related, she and Raederle, through the
witch Madir, in some obscure way they were trying
to figure out. The pig-woman's great gift was with
pigs; she was abrupt and shy with people, but the
beautiful, fiery Cyone had inherited Madir's interest in pigs and had become friends with the
taciturn pig-woman. But not even Cyone had discovered what Raederle knew: the odd store of
knowledge that the pig-woman had also inherited
from Madir.

Raederle picked another tough stem of grass,
sent it snaking in and out of the small, square
weave. "Am I doing this right?"

The pig-woman touched the tight strands and
nodded. "You could carry water in that," she said,
in her plain, rugged voice. "Now, then, I think
King Oen had a pigherder whom Madir might have
been fond of, in Anuin."

"I thought she might have been fond of Oen."

The pig-woman looked surprised. "After he built
the tower to trap her? You told me that. Besides, he
had a wife." She waved the words and her pipe
smoke away at once with her hand. "I'm not thinking."

"No king I ever heard of married Madir," Raederle said wryly. "Yet somehow the blood got into
the king's line. Let's see: she lived nearly two hun-

dred years, and there were seven kings. I believe
we can forget Fenel; he was too busy fighting almost to father a land-heir, let alone a bastard. I
don't even know if he kept pigs. It is possible," she
added, struck, "that you are a descendant of a child
of Madir and one of the Kings."

The pig-woman gave a rare chuckle. "Oh, I
doubt it. Me with my bare feet. Madir liked pig-
herders as much as she liked kings."

"That's true." She finished with the grass blade
and pushed the stems close, frowning down at them
absently. "It is also possible that Oen might have
grown fond of Madir after he realized she wasn't
his enemy, but that seems a little scandalous, since
it was through him that Ylon's blood came into the
Kings' line. Oen was furious enough about that."

"Ylon."

"You know that tale."

The pig-woman shook her head. "I know the
name, but no one ever told me the tale."

"Well." She sat back against the tree trunk, the
sun shimmering in and out of her eyes. Her own
shoes were off; her hair was loose; and there was a
small spider making a bewildered foray up one
strand. She brushed it off without noticing. "It's the
first riddle I ever learned. Oen's land-heir was not
his own son, but the son of some strange sea-lord,
who came into Oen's bed disguised as the king. Nine
months afterward, Oen's wife bore Ylon, with skin
like foam and eyes like green seaweed. So Oen in his
anger built a tower by the sea for this sea-child, with
orders that he should never come out of it. One
night, fifteen years after his birth, Ylon heard a
strange harping from the sea, and such was his love
of it, and desire to find its source, that he broke
the bars on his window with his hands and leaped
into the sea and vanished. Ten years later Oen
died, and to his other sons' surprise, the land-

rule passed to Ylon. Ylon was driven by his own nature back to claim his heritage. He reigned only long enough to marry and beget a son who was as dark and practical as Oen, and then he went back to the tower Oen had built for him and leaped to his death on the rocks below." She touched the tiny net, squared a corner. "It's a sad tale." A frown strayed into her eyes, absent, puzzled, as if she had almost remembered something, but not quite. "Anyway, Ylon's face appears once or twice a century, and sometimes his wildness, but never his terrible torment, because no one with his nature has ever again inherited the land-rule. Which is fortunate."

"That's true." The pig-woman looked down at the pipe in her hand, which had gone out during her listening. She tapped it absently against the tree root. Raederle watched an enormous black sow nudge her way through the clearing in front of them to loll panting in the shade.

"It's almost Dis's time."

The pig-woman nodded. "They'll all be black as pots, too, sired by Dark Noon."

Raederle spotted the boar responsible, the great descendant of Hegdis-Noon, rooting among the old leaves. "Maybe she'll bear one who can talk."

"Maybe. I keep hoping, but the magic, I think, has gone out of the blood and they are born silent."

"I wish a few of the Lords of An had been born silent."

The pig-woman's brows flicked up in sudden comprehension. "That's it, then."

"What?"

She shifted, shy again. "The spring council. It's nothing of my business, but I didn't think you had ridden for three days to find out if we were first or third cousins."

Raederle smiled. "No. I ran away from home."

"You . . . Does your father know where you are?"

"I always assume he knows everything." She reached for another stem of grass. The odd, tentative frown moved again into her face; she looked up suddenly to meet the pig-woman's eyes. For a moment, the direct, grey gaze seemed a stranger's look, curious, measuring, with the same question in it that she had barely put words to. Then the pig-woman's head bowed; she reached down to pick an acorn out of an angle of root and tossed it to the black sow. Raederle said softly, "Ylon . . ."

"He's why you can do these small things I teach you so well. He and Madir. And your father with his mind."

"Maybe. But—" She shook the thought away and leaned back again to breathe the tranquil air. "My father could see a shadow in a barrow, but I wish he didn't have a mouth like a clam. It's good to be away from that house. It grew so quiet last winter I thought whatever words we spoke would freeze solid in the air. I thought that winter would never end . . ."

"It was a bad one. The Lord had to send for feed from Aum and pay double because Aum itself was growing short of corn. We lost some of the herd; one of the great boars, Aloil—"

"Aloil?"

The pig-woman looked suddenly a little flustered. "Well, Rood mentioned him once, and I thought— I liked the name."

"You named a boar after a wizard?"

"Was he? I didn't . . . Rood didn't say. Anyway, he died in spite of all I could do for him, and the Lord himself even came to help with his own hands."

Raederle's face softened slightly. "Yes. That's one thing Raith is good with."

"It's in his blood. But he was upset about—about Aloil." She glanced at Raederle's handiwork. "You might want to make it a little wider, but you'll need to leave a fringe to hold it after you throw it."

Raederle stared down at the tiny net, watching it grow big then small again in her mind's eye. She reached for more grass, and felt, as her hand touched the earth, the steady drum of hoofbeats. She glanced, startled, toward the trees. "Who is that? Hasn't Raith left for Anuin yet?"

"No, he's still here. Didn't you—" She stopped as Raederle rose, cursing succinctly, and the Lord of Hel and his retinue came into the clearing, scattering pig.

Raith brought his mount to a halt in front of Raederle; his men, in pale green and black, drew to a surprised, disorderly stop. He stared down at her, his gold brows pulling quickly into a disapproving frown, and opened his mouth; she said, "You're going to be late for the council."

"I had to wait for Elieu. Why in Hel's name are you running around in your stockinged feet in my pig herds? Where is your escort? Where—"

"Elieu!" Raederle cried to a brown-bearded stranger dismounting from his horse, and his happy smile, as she ran to hug him, made him once again familiar.

"Did you get the flute I sent to you?" he asked, as she gripped his arms; she nodded, laughing.

"You sent it? Did you make it? It was so beautiful it frightened me."

"I wanted to surprise you, not—"

"I didn't recognize you in that beard. You haven't been out of Isig for three years; it's about time you—" She checked suddenly, her hold tightening. "Elieu, did you bring any news of the Prince of Hed?"

"I'm sorry," he said gently. "No one has seen him.

I sailed down from Kraal on a trade-ship; it stopped five times along the way, and I lost count long ago of how many people I had to tell that to. There is one thing, though, that I came to tell your father." He smiled again, touched her face. "You are always so beautiful. Like An itself. But what are you doing alone in Raith's pig herds?"

"I came to talk to his pig-woman, who is a very wise and interesting woman."

"She is?" Elieu looked at the pig-woman, who looked down at her feet.

Raith said grimly, "I would have thought you had outgrown such things. It was foolish of you to ride alone from Anuin; I'm amazed that your father —He does know where you are?"

"He has probably made a fairly accurate guess."

"You mean you—"

"Oh, Raith, if I want to make a fool of myself that's my business."

"Well, look at you! Your hair looks as though birds have been nesting in it."

Her hand rose impulsively to smooth it, then dropped. "That," she said frostily, "is also my business."

"It's beneath your dignity to consort with my pig-woman like some—like some—"

"Well, Raith, we are related. For all I know she has as much right in the court at Anuin as I have."

"I didn't know you were related," Elieu said interestedly. "How?"

"Madir. She was a busy woman."

Raith drew a long breath through his nose. "You," he said ponderously, "need a husband." He jerked his reins, turning his mount; at his straight, powerful back and rigorous movements something desperate, uneasy, touched Raederle. She felt Elieu's hand on her shoulder.

"Never mind," he said soothingly. "Will you

ride back with us? I would love to hear you play that flute."

"All right." Her shoulders slumped a little. "All right. If you're there. But first tell me what news you have to tell my father that brought you all the way down from Isig."

"Oh." She heard the sudden awe in his voice. "It's about the Prince—about the Star-Bearer."

Raederle swallowed. As if the pigs themselves had recognized the name, there was a lull in their vigorous snortings. The pig-woman looked up from her feet. "Well, what?"

"It was something Bere, Danan's grandson, told me. You must have heard the tale about Morgon, about the night he took the sword from the secret places of Isig, the night he killed three shape-changers with it, saving himself and Bere. Bere and I were working together, and Bere asked me what the Earth-Masters were. I told him as much as I knew, and asked him why. And he told me then that he had heard Morgon telling Danan and Deth that in the Cave of the Lost Ones, where no one had ever gone but Yrth, Morgon found his starred sword, and it had been given to him by the dead children of the Earth-Masters."

The pig-woman dropped her pipe. She rose in a swift, blurred movement that startled Raederle. The vagueness dropped from her face like a mask, revealing a strength and sorrow worn into it by a knowledge of far more than Raith's pigs. She drew a breath and shouted, "What?"

The shout cracked like lightning out of the placid sky. Raederle, flinging her arms futilely over her ears, heard above her own cry the shrill, terrified cries of rearing horses, and the breathless, gasping voices of men struggling to control them. Then came a sound as unexpected and terrible as the pig-

14

woman's shout: the agonized, outraged protest of the entire pig herd of Hel.

Raederle opened her eyes. The pig-woman had vanished, as though she had been blown away by her shout. The unwieldy, enormous pig herd, squealing with pain and astonishment, was heaving to its feet, turning blindly, massing like a great wave, panic rippling to the far edges of the herd in the distance. She saw the great boars wheeling, their eyes closed, the young pigs half-buried in the heave of bristled backs, the sows, huge with their unborn, swaying to their feet. The horses, appalled by the strange clamor and the pigs jostling against them, were wrenching out of control. One of them stepped back onto a small pig, and the double screech of terror from both animals sounded across the clearing like a battle horn. Hooves pounding, voices shrilling and snorting, the pride of Hel for nine centuries surged forward, dragging men and horses helplessly with them. Raederle, taking prompt, undignified shelter up the oak tree, saw Raith trying desperately to turn his horse and reach her. But he was swept away with his retinue, Elieu, whooping with laughter, bringing up the rear. The herd ebbed away and vanished into the distant trees. Raederle, straddling a bough, her head beginning to ache with the aftermath of the shout, thought of the pigs running along with the Lord of Hel all the way into the King's council hall in Anuin, and she laughed until she cried.

She found, riding wearily back into her father's courtyard at twilight three days later, that some of the pigs had gotten there before her. The inner walls were blazoned with the banners of the lords who had arrived; beneath the banner of Hel, limp in the evening air, were penned seven exhausted boars. She had to stop and laugh again, but the laughter was more subdued as she realized that she had to face Mathom. She wondered, as a groom ran to take her horse, why, with all the people in the house, it was so quiet. She went up the steps, into the open doors of the hall; amid the long lines of empty tables and the sprawl of chairs, there were only three people: Elieu, Duac and the King.

She said a little hesitantly as they turned at her step, "Where is everyone?"

"Out," Mathom said succinctly. "Looking for you."

"Your whole council?"

"My whole council. They left five days ago; they are probably scattered, like Raith's pigs, all over the Three Portions of An. Raith himself was last seen trying to herd his pigs together in Aum." His voice was testy, but there was no anger in his eyes, only a hiddenness, as if he were contemplating an entirely different train of thought. "Did it occur to you that anyone might be worried?"

"If you ask me," Duac murmured into his wine cup, "it seemed more like a hunting party than a search party, to see who would bring home the prize." Something in his face told Raederle that he and Mathom had been arguing again. He lifted his head. "You let them go like a cageful of freed birds. You can control your own lords better than that. I've never seen such shambles made of a council in my life, and you wanted it so. Why?"

Raederle sat down next to Elieu, who gave her a cup of wine and a smile. Mathom was standing; he made a rare, impatient gesture at Duac's words. "Does it occur to you that I might have been worried?"

"You weren't surprised when you heard she was gone. You didn't tell me to go after her, did you? No. You're more interested in sending me to Caithnard. While you do what?"

"Duac!" Mathom snapped, exasperated, and

Duac shifted in his chair. The King turned a dour eye to Raederle. "And I told you to stay out of Hel. You had a remarkable effect on both Raith's pigs and my council."

"I'm sorry. But I told you I needed to get out of this house."

"That badly? Riding precipitously off into Hel and back without an escort?"

"Yes."

She heard him sigh.

"How can I command obedience from my land when I cannot even rule my own household?" The question was rhetorical, for he exacted over his land and his house what he chose.

Duac said with dogged, weary patience, "If you would try explaining yourself for once in your life, it would make a difference. Even I will obey you. Try telling me in simple language why you think it is so imperative for me to bring Rood home. Just tell me. And I'll go."

"Are you still arguing about that?" Raederle said. She looked curiously at their father. "Why do you want Duac to bring Rood home? Why did you want me to stay out of Hel, when you know I am as safe on Raith's lands as in my garden?"

"Either," Mathom said tersely, "you, Duac, bring Rood home from Caithnard, or I will send a ship and a simple command to him. Which do you think he would prefer?"

"But why—"

"Let him puzzle his own brain about it. He's trained to answer riddles, and it will give him something to do."

Duac brought his hands together, linked them tightly. "All right," he said tautly. "All right. But I'm no riddler and I like things explained to me. Until you explain to me precisely why you want the one who will become my land-heir if you die

17

back here with me, I swear by Madir's bones that I'll see the wraiths of Hel ride across this threshold before I call Rood back to Anuin."

There was a chilling leap of pure anger in Mathom's face that startled Raederle. Duac's face lost nothing of its resolve, but she saw him swallow. Then his hands pulled apart, lowered to grip the table edge. He whispered, "You're leaving An."

In the silence, Raederle heard the far, faint bickering of sea gulls. She felt something hard, a word left in her from the long winter, melt away. It brought the tears for a moment into her eyes so that Mathom blurred to a shadow when she looked at him. "You're going to Erlenstar Mountain. To ask about the Prince of Hed. Please. I would like to come with you."

"No." But the voice of the shadow was gentle.

Elieu's head was moving slowly from side to side. He breathed, "Mathom, you can't. Anyone with even half a mind to reason with must realize—"

"That what he is contemplating," Duac interrupted, "is hardly a simple journey to Erlenstar Mountain and back." He rose, his chair protesting against the stones. "Is it?"

"Duac, at a time when the air itself is an ear, I do not intend to babble my business to the world."

"I am not the world. I am your land-heir. You've never been surprised once in your life, not when Morgon won that game with Peven, not even at Elieu's news of the waking of the children of the Earth-Masters. Your thoughts are calculated like a play on a chessboard, but I don't think even you know exactly who you are playing against. If all you want to do is to go to Erlenstar Mountain, you would not be sending for Rood. You don't know where you are going, do you? Or what you will find, or when you will get back? And you knew that if the Lords of the Three Portions were here listening to this, there would be an uproar that would shake the stones loose in the ceiling. You'll leave me to face the uproar, and you'll sacrifice the peace of your land for something that is not your concern but the business of Hed and the High One."

"The High One." Something harsh, unpleasant in the King's voice made the name almost unfamiliar. "Morgon's own people scarcely know a world exists beyond Hed, and except for one incident, I would wonder if the High One knows that Morgon exists."

"It's not your concern! You are liable to the High One for the rule of An, and if you let loose of the bindings in the Three Portions—"

"I don't need to be reminded of my responsibilities!"

"You can stand there plotting to leave An indefinitely and tell me that!"

"Is it possible that you can trust me when I weigh two things in the balance and find one looming more heavily than a momentary confusion in An?"

"Momentary confusion!" Duac breathed. "If you leave An too long, stray too far away from it, you will throw this land into chaos. If your hold on the things you bind in the Three Portions loosens, you'll find the dead kings of Hel and Aum laying siege to Anuin, and Peven himself wandering into this hall looking for his crown. If you return at all. And if you vanish, as Morgon did, for some long, wearisome length of time, this land will find itself in a maelstrom of terror."

"It's possible," Mathom said. "So far in its long history An has had nothing more challenging to fight than itself. It can survive itself."

"What worse can happen to it than such a chaos of living and dead?" He raised his voice, battering in anger and desperation against the King's implacability. "How can you think of doing this to your land? You don't have the right! And if you're not careful, you'll no longer have the land-rule."

Elieu leaned forward, gripped his arm. Raederle stood up, groping for words to quiet them. Then she caught sight of a stranger entering the hall, who had stopped abruptly at Duac's shout. He was young, plainly dressed in sheepskin and rough wool. He glanced in wonder at the beautiful hall, then stared a little at Raederle without realizing it. The numb, terrible sorrow in his eyes made her heart stop. She took a step towards him, feeling as though she were stepping irrevocably out of the predictable world. Something in her face had stopped the quarrel. Mathom turned. The stranger shifted uneasily and cleared his throat.

"I'm—my name is Cannon Master. I farm the lands of the Prince of Hed. I have a message for the King of An from—from the Prince of Hed."

"I am Mathom of An."

Raederle took another step forward. "And I am Raederle," she whispered, while something fluttered, trapped like a bird, in the back of her throat. "Is Morgon . . . Who is the Prince of Hed?"

She heard a sound from Mathom. Cannon Master looked at her mutely a moment. Then he said very gently, "Eliard."

Into their incredulous silence, the King dropped one word like a stone. "How?"

"No one—no one knows exactly." He stopped to swallow. "All Eliard knows is that Morgon died five days ago. We don't know how, or where, only that it was under very strange and terrible circumstances. Eliard knows that much because he has been dreaming about Morgon the past year, feeling something—some nameless power weighing into Morgon's mind. He couldn't—he couldn't seem to free himself from it. He didn't even seem to know himself at the end. We can't begin to guess what it was. Five days ago, the land-rule passed to Eliard. We remembered the reason why Morgon had left Hed in the first place, and we—Eliard decided . . ." He paused; a faint flush of color came into his weary face. He said diffidently to Raederle, "I don't know if you would have chosen to come to Hed. You would have been—you would have been most welcome. But we thought it right that you should be told. I had been once to Caithnard, so I said I'd come."

"I see." She tried to clear the trembling in her throat. "Tell him—tell him I would have come. I would have come."

His head bowed. "Thank you for that."

"A year," Duac whispered. "You knew what was happening to him. You knew. Why didn't you tell someone? Why didn't you let us know sooner?"

Cannon Master's hands clenched. He said painfully, "It's what—it's what we ask ourselves now. We—we just kept hoping. No one of Hed has ever asked outside of Hed for help."

"Has there been any word from the High One?" Elieu asked.

"No. Nothing. But no doubt the High One's harpist will show up eventually to express the High One's sorrow over the death of—" He stopped, swallowing the bitterness from his voice. "I'm sorry. We can't—we can't even bury him in his own land. I'm ignorant as a sheep outside of Hed; I hardly know, stepping out of your house, which direction to turn to go home. So I have to ask you if, beyond Hed, such things happen to land-rulers so frequently that not even the High One is moved by it."

Duac stirred, but Mathom spoke before he could. "Never," he said flatly. Cannon, drawn by something smoldering in his eyes, took a step toward the King, his voice breaking.

"Then what was it? Who killed him? Where, if the High One himself doesn't care, can we go for an answer?"

The King of An looked as though he were swallowing a shout that might have blown the windows out of the room. He said succinctly, "I swear by the bones of the unconquered Kings of An, that if I have to bring it back from the dead I will find you an answer."

Duac dropped his face in one hand. "You've done it now." Then he shouted, while Cannon stared at him, amazed, "And if you go wandering through this realm like a peddlar and that darkness that killed Morgon snatches you out of time and place, don't bother troubling me with your dreams because I won't look for you!"

"Then look to my land," Mathom said softly. "Duac, there is a thing in this realm that eats the minds of land-rulers, that is heaving restlessly under the earth with more hatred in it than even in the bones of the dead of Hel. And when it rouses at last, there will not be a blade of grass in this land untouched by it."

He vanished so quickly that Duac started. He stood staring at the air where Mathom had gone out like a dark, windblown flame. Cannon said, appalled, "I'm sorry—I'm sorry—I never dreamed—"

"It wasn't your fault," Elieu said gently. His face was bloodless. He put a hand on Raederle's wrist; she looked at him blindly. He added to Duac, "I'll stay in Hel. I'll do what I can."

Duac ran his hands up his face, up through his hair. "Thank you." He turned to Cannon. "You can believe him. He'll find out who killed Morgon and why, and he'll tell you if he has to drag him-

self out of a grave to do it. He has sworn that, and
he is bound beyond life."

Cannon shuddered. "Things are much simpler in
Hed. Things die when they're dead."

"I wish they did in An."

Raederle, staring out at the darkening sky beyond the windows, touched his arm suddenly.
"Duac . . ."

An old crow swung over the garden on a drift
of wind, then flapped northward over the rooftops
of Anuin. Duac's eyes followed it as though something in him were bound to the deliberate, unhur-
ried flight. He said wearily, "I hope he doesn't get
himself shot and cooked for dinner."

Cannon looked at him, startled. Raederle, watching the black wings shirr the blue-grey twilight,
said, "Someone should go to Caithnard to tell
Rood. I'll go." Then she put her hands over her
mouth and began to cry for a young student in the
White of Beginning Mastery who had once put a
shell to her ear so she could hear the sea.

2

S HE REACHED CAITHNARD FOUR DAYS LATER. THE sea, green and white as Ylon's memory, rolled her father's ship into the harbor with an exuberant twist of froth, and she disembarked, after it anchored, with relief. She stood watching sailors unload sacks of seed, plowhorses, sheepskins and wool from the ship next to them; and, farther down, from a ship trimmed in orange and gold, strong, shaggy-hooved horses and gilded chests. Her own horse was brought to her; her father's ship-master, Bri Corbett, came down finally, issuing reminders to the crew all the way down the ramp, to escort her to the College. He swivelled an eye bleak as an oyster at a sailor who was gaping at Raederle from under a grain sack, and the sailor shut his mouth. Then he took the reins of their mounts, began threading a slow path through the crowded docks.

"There's Joss Merle, down from Osterland, I'll wager," he said, and pointed out to Raederle a low, wide-bellied ship with pine-colored sails. "Packed to the boom with furs. Why he doesn't spin circles in that tub, I'll never know. And there's Halster

Tull, there, on the other side of the orange ship. Your pardon, Lady. To a man who was once a trader, being at Caithnard in spring is like being in your father's wine cellar with an empty cup; you don't know where to look first."

She smiled a little and realized, from the stiffness of her face, how long it had been since she had last done it. "I like hearing about them," she said politely, knowing her silence during the past days had worried him. A cluster of young women were chattering at the ramp of the orange and yellow ship in front of them. Their long, elegant robes wove, glinting, with the air; they seemed to be pointing every conceivable direction, their faces bright with excitement as they talked, and her smile deepened slightly. "Whose is the orange ship?"

The ship-master opened his mouth. Then he closed it again, frowning. "I've never seen it before. But I would swear . . . No. It couldn't be."

"What?"

"The Morgol's guards. She so rarely leaves Herun."

"Who are?"

"Those young women. Pretty as flowers, but show one of them the wrong side of your hand and you'd wind up in the water halfway to Hed." He cleared his throat uncomfortably. "Your pardon."

"Don't talk about crows, either."

"No." Then he shook his head slowly. "A crow. And I would have sailed him with my own hands, if need be, clear up the Ose to Erlenstar Mountain."

She stepped around a precarious stack of wine kegs. Her eyes slid suddenly to his face. "Could you? Take my father's ship all the way up the Ose?"

"Well. No. There's not a ship in the world that

could take the Pass, with all its rapids and falls. But I would have tried, if he'd asked me."

"How far could he have gone by ship?"

"To Kraal, by sea, then up the Winter River to join with the Ose near Isig. But it's a slow journey upriver, especially in spring when the snow waters are making for the sea. And you'd need a shorter keel than your father's ship has."

"Oh."

"It's a broad, placid river, the Winter, to the eye, but it can shift ground so much in a year you'd swear you were sailing a different river. It's like your father; you never quite know what it's going to do next." He flushed deeply, but she only nodded, watching the forest of genially bobbing masts.

"Devious."

They mounted when they reached the street and rode through the bustling city, up the road that wound above the white beaches to the ancient College. There were a few students sprawled on the ground, reading with their chins on their fists; they did not bother to look up until the ship-master made the rare gesture of knocking. A student in the Red with a harried expression on his face swung open the door and inquired rather abruptly of his business.

"We have come to see Rood of An."

"If I were you, I would try a tavern. The Lost Sailor, by the wharf, is a good bet, or the King's Oyster—" He saw Raederle, then, mounted behind the ship-master, and took a step toward her. "I'm sorry, Raederle. Will you come in and wait?"

She put a name finally to the lean, red-haired riddler. "Tes. I remember. You taught me how to whistle."

His face broke into a pleased smile. "Yes. I was in the Blue of Partial Beginning, and you were—

you . . . Anyway," he added at the ship-master's expression, "the Masters' library is empty, if you would care to wait."

"No, thank you," she said. "I know where the Lost Sailor is, but where is the King's Oyster?"

"On Cutters Street. You remember; it used to be the Sea-Witch's Eye."

"Who," Bri Corbett barked, "in Hel's name do you think you're talking to? How would she know the name or whereabouts of any inn or tavern in any city anywhere in this realm?"

"I know," Raederle said with some asperity, "because every time I come here Rood either has his nose in a book or a cup. I was hoping this time it would be a book." She stopped, then, uneasy, crumpling the reins in her hands. "Has he—have you heard the news out of Hed?"

"Yes." His head bowed; he repeated softly, "Yes. A trader brought the news last night. The College is in a turmoil. I haven't seen Rood since then, and I've been up all night with the Masters." She sighed, and his head came up. "I would help you look, but I'm due down at the docks to escort the Morgol to the College."

"It's all right. We'll find him."

"I'll find him," Bri Corbett said with emphasis. "Please, Lady, the Caithnard taverns are no place for you."

She turned her horse. "Having a father flying around in the shape of a crow gives you a certain disregard for appearances. Besides, I know which ones are his favorites."

They looked in them all without success. By the time they had asked a half a dozen of them, they had an eager following of young students who knew Rood, and who went through each tavern with methodical and startling thoroughness. Raederle, watching them through a window as they

checked under the tables, murmured in amazement, "When does he find time to study?"

Bri Corbett took off his hat, fanned his sweating face with it. "I don't know. Let me take you
back to the ship."

"No."

"You're tired. And you must be hungry. And
your father will trim my sails for me if he ever
hears of this. I'll find Rood and bring him to the
ship."

"I want to find him. I want to talk to him."

The students jostled without their quarry back
out of the inn. One of them called to her, "The
Heart's Hope Inn on Fish-Market Street. We'll try
that."

"Fish-Market Street?"

"The south horn of the harbor. You might," he
added thoughtfully, "want to wait for us here."

"I'll come," she said.

The street, under the hot eye of the afternoon
sun, seemed to shimmer with the smell of fish lying
gutted and glassy-eyed in the market stalls. The
ship-master groaned softly. Raederle, thinking of
the journey they had made from the contemplative
peace of the College through the maze of Caithnard to the most noisome street in the city, littered
with assorted fishheads, backbones and spitting
cats, began to laugh weakly.

"Heart's Hope Inn . . ."

"There it is," Bri Corbett said heavily as the students disappeared into it. He seemed almost beyond speech. The inn was small, tired, settling on
its hindquarters with age, but beyond its dirty,
mullioned windows there seemed to be an unwar-
ranted, very colorful collage of activity. The ship-
master put his hand on the neck of Raederle's
mount. He looked at her. "No more. I'll take you
back now."

She stared wearily at the worn stone threshold of the inn. "I don't know where else to look. Maybe the beaches. I want to find him, though. Sometimes there's one thing worse than knowing precisely what Rood is thinking, and that's not knowing what he's thinking."

"I'll find him, I swear it. You—" The inn door opened abruptly, and he turned his head. One of the students who had been helping them was precipitated bodily to the cobble-stones under the nose of Bri Corbett's horse. He staggered to his feet and panted, "He's there."

"Rood?" Raederle exclaimed.

"Rood." He touched a corner of his bleeding mouth with the tip of his tongue and added, "You should see it. It's awesome."

He flung the door wide and plunged back into a turmoil of color, a maelstrom of blue, white and gold that whirled and collided against a flaming core of red. The ship-master stared at it almost wistfully. Raederle dropped her face in her hands. Then she slid tiredly off her horse. A robe of Intermediate Mastery, minus its wearer, shot out over her head, drifted to a gold puddle on the stones. She went to the door, the noise in the tavern drowning the ship-master's sudden, gargled protest. Rood was surfacing in his bright, torn robe from the heaving tangle of bodies.

His face looked meditative, austere, in spite of the split on one cheekbone, as if he were quietly studying instead of dodging fists in a tavern brawl. She watched, fascinated, as a goose, plucked and headless, flapped across the air above his head and thumped into a wall. Then she called to him. He did not hear her, one of his knees occupying the small of a student's back while he shook another, a little wiry student in the White, off his arm onto the outraged inn-keeper. A powerful student in the

Gold, with a relentless expression on his face, caught Rood from behind by the neck and one wrist, and said politely, "Lord, will you stop before I take you apart and count your bones?" Rood, blinking a little at the grip on his neck, moved abruptly; the student loosed him and sat down slowly on the wet floor, bent over himself and gasping. There was a general attack then, from the small group of students who had come with Raederle. Raederle, wincing, lost sight of Rood again; he rose finally near her, breathing deeply, his hands full of a brawny fisherman who looked as massive and impervious as the great White Bull of Aum. Rood's fist, catching him somewhere under his ribs, barely troubled him. Raederle watched while he gathered the throat of Rood's robe in one great hand, clenched the other and drew it back, and then she lifted a wine flagon in her hand, one that she could not remember picking up, and brought it down on the head of the bull.

He let go of Rood and sat down blinking in a shower of wine and glass. She stared down at him, appalled. Then she looked at Rood, who was staring at her.

His stillness spread through the inn until only private, fierce struggles in corners still flared. He was, she saw with surprise, sober as a stone. Faces, blurred, battle-drunk, were turning towards her all over the room; the innkeeper, holding two heads he was about to bang together, was gazing at her, open-mouthed, and she thought of the dead, surprised fish in the stalls. She dropped the neck of the flagon; the clink of it breaking sounded frail in the silence. She flushed hotly and said to the statue that was Rood, "I'm sorry. I didn't mean to interrupt. But I've been looking all over Caithnard for you, and I didn't want him to hit you before I could talk to you."

He moved finally, to her relief. He turned, lost his balance briefly, caught it, and said to the innkeeper, "Send the bill to my father."

He stepped off the porch with a jar he must have felt to his teeth, reached for Raederle's horse and clung to it, his face against the saddlecloth a moment before he spoke to her. Then he lifted his head, blinked at her. "You're still here. I didn't think I'd been drinking. What in Hel's name are you doing standing in all those fishbones?"

"What in Hel's name do you think I'm doing here?" she demanded. Her voice, strained, low; let free finally all the grief, confusion and fear she felt. "I need you."

He straightened, slid an arm around her shoulders, held her tightly, and said to the ship-master, who had dropped his head in his hands and was shaking it, "Thank you. Will you send someone to take my things out of the College?"

Bri Corbett's head came up. "Everything, Lord?"

"Everything. Every dead word and dry wine stain in that room. Everything."

He took Raederle to a quiet inn in the heart of the city. Seated with a flagon of wine in front of them, he watched her drink in silence, his hands linked over his own cup. He said finally, softly, "I don't believe he is dead."

"Then what do you believe? That he was simply driven mad and lost the land-rule? That's a comforting thought. Is that why you were tearing that inn apart?"

He shifted, his eyes falling. "No." He reached out, put his hand on her wrist, and her fingers, molding the metal of her cup, loosened and came to rest on the table. She whispered, "Rood, that's the terrible thing I can't get out of my mind. That while I was waiting, while we were all waiting, safe and secure, thinking he was with the High One, he was alone with someone who was picking his mind apart as you would pick apart the petals of a closed flower. And the High One did nothing."

"I know. One of the traders brought the news up to the College yesterday. The Masters were stunned. Morgon unearthed such a vipers' nest of riddles, and then so inconveniently died without answering them. Which put the entire problem at their door, since the College exists to answer the answerable. The Masters are set face-to-face with their own strictures. This riddle is literally deadly, and they began wondering exactly how interested they are in truth." He took a sip of his wine, looked at her again. "Do you know what happened?"

"What?"

"Eight old Masters and nine Apprentices argued all night about who would travel to Erlenstar Mountain to speak to the High One. Every one of them wanted to go."

She touched the torn sleeve of his robe. "You're an Apprentice."

"No. I told Master Tel yesterday I was leaving. Then I—then I went to the beach and sat up all night, not doing anything, not even thinking. I came into Caithnard finally and stopped at that inn for something to eat, and while—while I was eating, I remembered an argument I had with Morgon before he left about not facing his own destiny, not living up to his own standards when all he wanted to do was make beer and read books. So he went and found his destiny in some remote corner of the realm, driven, by the sound of it, mad as Peven. So. I decided to take the inn apart. Nail by nail. And then go and answer the riddles he couldn't answer."

She gave a little, unsurprised nod. "I thought you

32

might. Well, that's another piece of news I have to give you."

He touched his cup again, said warily, "What?"

"Our father left An five days ago to do just that. He—" She winced as his hands went down sharply on the table, causing a trader at the next table to choke on his beer.

"He left An? For how long?"

"He didn't . . . He swore by the ancient Kings to find what it was that killed Morgon. That long. Rood, don't shout."

He swallowed it, rendered himself momentarily wordless. "The old crow."

"Yes . . . He left Duac at Anuin to explain to the lords. Our father was going to send for you to help Duac, but he wouldn't say why, and Duac was furious that he wanted you to abandon your studies."

"Did Duac send you to bring me home?"

She shook her head. "He didn't even want me to tell you. He swore that he wouldn't send for you until the wraiths of Hel crossed the threshold at Anuin."

"He did that?" Rood said with disgusted wonder. "He's getting as irrational as our father. He would have let me sit in Caithnard studying for a rank that suddenly has very little meaning while he tries to keep order among the living and dead of An. I'd rather go home and play riddle-games with the dead kings."

"Will you?"

"What?"

"Go home? It's a—it's a smaller thing to ask of you than going to Erlenstar Mountain, but Duac will need you. And our father—"

"Is a very capable and subtle old crow . . ." He was silent, frowning, his thumbnail picking at a flaw in his cup. He leaned back in his chair finally and sighed. "All right. I can't let Duac face that alone. At least I can be there to tell him which dead king is which, if nothing else. There's nothing I could do in Erlenstar Mountain that our father wouldn't do, and probably do better. I would give the Black of Mastery to see the world out of his eyes. But if he gets into trouble, I don't promise not to look for him."

"Good. Because that's another thing Duac said he wouldn't do."

His mouth crooked. "Duac seems to have lost his temper. I can't say that I blame him."

"Rood . . . Have you ever known our father to be wrong?"

"A hundred times."

"No. Not irritating, frustrating, annoying, incomprehensible and exasperating. Just wrong."

"Why?"

She shrugged slightly. "When he heard about Morgon—that's the first time in my life I can remember seeing him surprised. He—"

"What are you thinking about?" He leaned forward abruptly. "That vow he made to marry you to Morgon?"

"Yes. I always wondered a little, if it might have been foreknowledge. I thought maybe that's why he was so surprised."

She heard him swallow; his eyes, speculative, indrawn, reminded her of Mathom. "I don't know. I wonder. If so—"

"Then Morgon must be alive."

"But where? In what circumstances? And why in the name of the roots of the world won't the High One help him? That's the greatest riddle of them all: the miasma of silence coming out of that mountain."

"Well, if our father goes there, it won't be so silent." She shook her head wearily. "I don't know.

I don't know which to hope for. If he is alive, can you imagine what a stranger he must be even to himself? And he must—he must wonder why none of us who loved him tried to help him."

Rood opened his mouth, but the answer he would have given her seemed to wither on his tongue. He brought the heels of his hands up to his eyes. "Yes. I'm tired. If he is alive—"

"Our father will find him. You said you would help Duac."

"All right. But . . . All right." He dropped his hands, stared into his wine. Then he pushed his chair back slowly. "We'd better go; I have books to pack."

She followed him again into the bright, noisy street. It seemed, for a moment, to be flowing past her in a marvellous, incomprehensible pattern of color, and she stopped, blinking. Rood put a hand on her arm. She realized then that she had nearly stepped in front of a small, elegant procession. A woman led it. She sat tall and beautiful on a black mount, her dark hair braided and jewelled like a crown on her head, her light, shapeless green coat of some cloth that seemed to flow like a mist into the wind. Six young women whom Raederle had seen at the dock followed her in two lines, their robes, saddlecloths and reins of rich, vivid colors, their spears of ash inlaid with silver. One of them, riding close behind the Morgol, had the same black hair and fine, clean cast of face. Behind the guard came eight men on foot carrying two chests painted and banded with copper and gold; they were followed by eight students from the College, riding according to their ranks and the color of their robes: scarlet, gold, blue and white. The woman, riding as serenely through the press as through a meadow, glanced down suddenly as she passed the inn; at the brief, vague touch of the gold eyes,

Raederle felt the odd shock, unfamiliar and deep within her, of a recognition of power.

Rood breathed beside her, "The Morgol of Herun . . ."

He moved so quickly after the procession passed, gripping her wrist and pulling her, that she nearly lost her balance. She protested, "Rood!" as he ran to catch up with it, tugging her past amazed spectators, but he was shouting himself.

"Tes! Tes!" He caught up finally, Raederle flushed and irritated behind him, with the red-robed scholar. Tes stared down at him.

"What did you do? Fall face first in an empty wine bottle?"

"Tes, let me take your place. Please." He caught at the reins, but Tes flicked them out of reach.

"Stop that. Do you want us to get out of pace? Rood, are you drunk?"

"No. I swear it. I'm sober as a dead man. She's bringing Iff's books; you can see them any time, but I'm going home tonight—"

"You're what?"

"I have to leave. Please."

"Rood," Tes said helplessly. "I would, but do you realize what you look like?"

"Change with me. Tes. Please. Please."

Tes sighed. He pulled up sharply, tangling the line of horsemen behind him, slid off his horse and pulled wildly at the buttons on his robe. Rood tore his own robe over his head and thrust himself into Tes's, while the riders behind them made caustic remarks about his assertion of sobriety. He leaped onto Tes's horse and reached down for Raederle.

"Rood, my horse—"

"Tes can ride it back up. It's the chestnut back there at the inn; the saddlecloth has her initials on it. Come up—" She put her foot on his in the stirrup and he pulled her urgently into the saddle in front of him, urging the horse into a quick trot to catch up with the second, receding line of scholars. He shouted back, "Tes, thank you!"

Raederle, clenching her teeth against the jog of cobblestones, refrained from comment until he had brought the small line of riders behind him back into the sedately moving procession. Then she said, shifting down from the hard edge of the saddle, "Do you have any idea of how ridiculous that must have looked?"

"Do you know what we're about to see? Private books of the wizard Iff, opened. The Morgol opened them herself. She's donating them to the College; the Masters have been talking of nothing else for weeks. Besides, I've always been curious about her. They say all information passes eventually through the Morgol's house and that the High One's harpist loves her."

"Deth?" She mulled over the thought curiously. "Then I wonder if she knows where he is. No one else seems to."

"If anyone does, she does."

Raederle was silent, remembering the strange insight she had glimpsed in the Morgol's eyes, and her own unexpected recognition of it. They left the noisy, crowded streets behind them gradually; the road widened, rising toward the high cliff and the dark, wind-battered college. The Morgol, glancing back, set a slower pace uphill for the men carrying the chests. Raederle, looping out over the ocean, saw Hed partly misted under a blue-grey spring storm. She wondered suddenly, intensely, as she had never wondered before, what lay at the heart of the small, simple island that it had produced out of its life and history the Star-Bearer. And then, briefly, it seemed she could see beneath the rain mists on the island to where a young man colored and thewed like an oak, was crossing the yard from a barn to a house, his yellow head bent under the rain.

She moved abruptly, murmuring; Rood put a hand up to steady her. "What's the matter?"

"Nothing. I don't know. Rood——"

"What?"

"Nothing."

One of the guards detached herself then from the line, rode back towards them. She turned her horse again to ride beside them in a single, flowing movement of mount and rider that seemed at once controlled and instinctive. She said politely, appraising them, "The Morgol, who was introduced to the students at the docks, is interested in knowing who joined her escort in place of Tes."

"I am Rood of An," Rood said. "This is my sister, Raederle. And I am—or I was until last night—an Apprentice at the College."

"Thank you." She paused a little, looking at Raederle; something young, oddly surprised, broke through the dark, preoccupied expression in her eyes. She added unexpectedly, "I am Lyraluthuin. The daughter of the Morgol."

She cantered back to the head of the procession. Rood, his eyes on the tall, lithe figure, gave a soft whistle.

"I wonder if the Morgol needs an escort back to Herun."

"You're going to Anuin."

"I could go to Anuin by way of Herun . . . She's coming back."

"The Morgol," Lyra said, rejoining them, "would like very much to speak with you."

Rood pulled out of line, following her up the hill. Raederle, sitting half-on and half-off the saddlebow, clinging to Rood and the horse's mane as she jounced, felt slightly silly. But the Morgol, her face lighting with a smile, seemed only pleased to see them.

"So you are Mathom's children," she said. "I have always wanted to meet your father. You joined my escort rather precipitously, and I did not expect at all to find in it the second most beautiful woman of An."

"I came to Caithnard to give Rood some news," Raederle said simply. The Morgol's smile faded; she nodded.

"I see. We heard the news only this morning, when we docked. It was unexpected." She looked at Rood. "Lyra tells me that you are no longer an Apprentice at the College. Have you lost faith in riddle-mastery?"

"No. Only my patience." His voice sounded husky; Raederle, glancing at him, found that he was blushing, as far as she knew, for the first time in his life.

The Morgol said softly, "Yes. So have I. I have brought seven of Iff's books and twenty others that have been collected in the library at the City of Circles through the centuries to give to the College, and a piece of news that, like the news from Hed, should stir even the dust in the Masters' library."

"Seven," Rood breathed. "You opened seven of Iff's books?"

"No. Only two. The wizard himself, the day that we left for Caithnard, opened the other five."

Rood wrenched at his reins; Raederle swayed against him. The guard behind him broke their lines abruptly to avoid bumping into him; the men bearing the chests came to a quick halt, and the students, who had not been paying attention, reined into one another, cursing. The Morgol stopped.

"Iff is alive?" He seemed oblivious of the mild chaos in his wake.

"Yes. He had hidden himself in my guard. He

had been in the Herun court, in one guise or another, for seven centuries, for he said it was, even in its earlier days, a place of scholarship. He said—" Her voice caught; they heard, when she continued, the rare touch of wonder in it. "He said he had been the old scholar who helped me to open those two books. When the scholar died, he became my falconer, and then a guard. But that he didn't care for. He took his own shape on the day they say Morgon died."

"Who freed him?" Rood whispered.

"He didn't know."

Raederle put her hands to her mouth, suddenly no longer seeing the Morgol's face, but the ancient, strong-boned face of the pig-woman of Hel, with the aftermath of a great and terrible darkness in her eyes.

"Rood," she whispered. "Raith's pig-woman. She heard some news Elieu brought from Isig about the Star-Bearer, and she shouted a shout that scattered the pig herds of Hel like thistledown. Then she disappeared. She named . . . she named one boar Aloil."

She heard the draw of his breath. "Nun?"

"Maybe the High One freed them.'"

"The High One." Something in the Morgol's tone, thoughtful as it was, reminded Raederle of Mathom. "I don't know why he would have helped the wizards and not the Star-Bearer, but I am sure, if that is the case, that he had his reasons." She glanced down the road, saw the lines in order and resumed her pace. They had nearly reached the top of the hill; the grounds, shadowed and gilded with oak leaves, stretched beyond the road's end.

Rood glanced at the Morgol, asked with unusual hesitancy, "May I ask you something?"

"Of course, Rood."

"Do you know where the High One's harpist is?"

The Morgol did not answer for a moment, her eyes on the bulky, rough-hewn building whose windows and doors were brilliant with color as the students crowded to watch her arrival. Then she looked down at her hands. "No. I have had no word from him."

The Masters came out, black as crows among the swirl of red and gold, to meet the Morgol. The chests were carried up to the library, the books examined lovingly by the Masters as they listened with wonder to the Morgol's tale of how she had opened the two. Raederle glanced at one set on the broad stand made for it. The black writing looked pinched and ascetic, but she found unexpectedly, turning a page, precise, delicate drawings of wild flowers down the margin. It made her think again of the pig-woman, smoking her pipe with her bare feet among the oak roots, and she smiled a little, wonderingly. Then the one still figure in the room caught her eye: Lyra, standing by the door in a habitual stance, her back straight, her feet apart, as if she were keeping watch over the room. But her eyes were smudged with a blackness, and she was seeing nothing.

The room fell silent as the Morgol told the Masters of the reappearance of the wizard Iff. She asked Raederle to repeat the tale of the pig-woman, and Raederle complied, giving them also the startling news that had brought Elieu down from Isig. That, no one had heard, not even the Morgol, and there was an outburst of amazement after she finished. They asked questions in their kind voices she could not answer; they asked questions among themselves no one could answer. Then the Morgol spoke again. What she said Raederle did not hear, only the silence that was passed like a tangible thing from Master to Master, from group to group in the room until there was not a sound in the room except one very old Master's breathing. The Morgol's expression had not changed; only her eyes had grown watchful.

"Master Ohm" said a frail, gentle Master whose name was Tel, "was with us at all times until last spring, when he journeyed to Lungold for a year of peaceful study and contemplation. He could have gone anywhere he wished; he chose the ancient city of the wizards. His letters to us have been carried by the traders from Lungold." He paused, his passionless, experienced eyes on her face. "El, you are as known and respected for your intelligence and integrity as is this College; if there is any criticism you would make of it, don't hesitate to tell us."

"It is the integrity of the College that I question, Master Tel," the Morgol said softly, "in the person of Master Ohm, who I doubt you will ever see within these walls again. And I question the intelligence of us all, myself included. Shortly before I left Herun, I had a visit from the King of Osterland, who came very simply and privately. He wondered if I had news of Morgon of Hed. He said he had gone to Isig, but not to Erlenstar Mountain, for the mists and storms were terrible through the Pass, too terrible even for a vesta. While he was with me, he told me something that reinforced suspicions that I have had since my last visit here. He said that Morgon had told him that the last word the wizard Suth had spoken as he lay dying in Morgon's arms, was Ohm's name. Ohm. Ghisteslwchlohm. The Founder of Lungold, Suth accused with his last breath." She paused, her eyes moving from face to motionless face. "I asked Har if he had taken the question to the College, and he laughed and said that the Masters of Knowledge could recognize neither the Star-Bearer nor the Founder of Lungold."

She paused again, but there was no protest, no

excuse from the men listening. Her head bowed slightly. "Master Ohm has been in Lungold since spring. The High One's harpist has not been seen since then, and from all accounts, the High One himself has been silent since then. The death of the Prince of Hed freed the wizards from the power held over them. I suggest that the Founder of Lungold freed the wizards because in killing the Star-Bearer, he no longer needed to fear their power or interference. I also suggest that if this College is to continue to justify its existence, it should examine, very carefully and very quickly, the heart of this impossible, imperative tangle of riddles."

There was a sound like a sigh through the room; it was the sea wind, searching the walls, like a bird, to get free. Lyra turned abruptly; the door had closed behind her before anyone realized she had moved. The Morgol's eyes flicked to the door, then back to the Masters, who had begun to speak again, their voices murmuring, hushed. They began to group themselves around the Morgol. Rood stood with his hands flat on one of the desks, leaning over a book, but his face was bloodless, his shoulders rigid, and Raederle knew he was not seeing it. Raederle took a step towards him. Then she turned, eased through the Masters to the door and went out.

She passed students in the hall waiting, eager and curious, for a glimpse of the books; she scarcely heard their voices. She barely felt the wind, grown cool and restless in the early spring dusk, pulling at her as she walked through the grounds. She saw Lyra standing beneath a tree at the cliff's edge, her back to the College. Something in the taut set of her shoulders, her bowed head, drew Raederle towards her. As she crossed the grounds, Lyra's spear lifted, spun a circle of light in the air, and plunged point down into the earth.

She turned at a rustle of leaf she heard under the rustle of wind-tossed trees. Raederle stopped. They looked at one another silently. Then Lyra, giving shape to the grief and anger in her eyes, said almost challengingly, "I would have gone with him. I would have protected him with my life."

Raederle's eyes moved away from her to the sea . . . the sea far below them, the half-moon of harbor it had hollowed, the jut of land to the north beyond which lay other lands, other harbors. Her hands closed. "My father's ship is here at Caithnard. I can take it as far as Kraal. I want to go to Erlenstar Mountain. Will you help me?"

Lyra's lips parted. Raederle saw a brief flash of surprise and uncertainty in her face. Then she gripped her spear, pulled it again out of the earth and gave a little emphatic nod. "I'll come."

3

WHEN LYRA TOOK THE MORGOL'S GUARDS INTO Caithnard later that evening to look for lodgings, Raederle followed them. She had left, in front of Rood's horse in the College stable, a small tangle of bright gold thread she had loosened from her cuff. Within the tangle, in her mind, she had placed her name and an image of Rood stepping on it, or his horse, and then riding without thought every curve and twist of thread through the streets of Caithnard until, reaching the end, he would blink free of the spell and find that neither the ship nor the tide had waited for him. He would suspect her, she knew, but there would be nothing he could do but ride back to Anuin, while Bri Corbett, under the urgings of the Morgol's guard, sailed north.

The guard had not been told. She heard fragments of their conversation, their laughter under the hollow, restless boom of the sea as she rode behind them down the hill. It was nearly dark; the wind dulled her horse's steps, but still she kept, as Lyra had advised, a distance between her and the guard. She felt, all the way into Caithnard, the touch of the Morgol's eyes at her back.

She caught up with the guard at a quiet side street near the docks. They were looking a little bewildered; one girl said, "Lyra, there's nothing but warehouses here." Lyra, without answering, turned her head and saw Raederle. Raederle met her brief, searching gaze, then Lyra looked at the guard. Something in her face quieted them. Her hand tightened and loosened on her spear. Then she lifted her chin.

"I am leaving tonight for Erlenstar Mountain with Raederle of An. I am doing this without permission from the Morgol; I am deserting the guard. I couldn't protect the Prince of Hed while he was alive; all I can do now is find out from the High One who killed him and where that one is. We're sailing to Kraal in her father's ship. The shipmaster has not yet been informed. I can't . . . Wait a minute. I can't ask you to help me. I can't hope that you would do such a shameful, disgraceful thing as leaving the Morgol alone, unguarded in a strange city. I don't know how I can do it. But what I do know is that we can't steal a ship by ourselves."

There was a silence when she stopped, but for a door rattling back and forth somewhere in the wind. The guards' faces were expressionless. Then one of them, a girl with a silky blond braid and a sweet, sunburned face, said fiercely, "Lyra, are you out of your mind?" She looked at Raederle. "Are you both out of your minds?"

"No," Raederle said. "There's not a trader in the realm who would take us, but my father's shipmaster has already half an inclination to go. He could never be persuaded, but he could be forced. He respects you, and once he grasps the situation, I don't think he'll argue much."

"But what will the Morgol say? What will your own people say?"

"I don't know. I don't care."

The girl shook her head, speechless. "Lyra—"

"Imer, you have three choices. You can leave us here and go back to the College and inform the Morgol. You can take us by force back to the College, which would greatly exceed your duty and would offend the people of An, not to mention me. You can come with us. The Morgol has twenty guards waiting in Hlurle to escort her back to Crown City; all she has to do is send word to them, and they'll join her at Caithnard. She'll be safe. What she will say to you, however, if she finds that you have let me go off by myself to Erlenstar Mountain, I would not like to hear."

Another girl, with a dark, plain face, and the rough timbre of the Herun hill towns in her voice, said reasonably, "She'll think we've all deserted."

"Goh, I'll tell her it was my responsibility."

"You can hardly tell her you coerced us all. Lyra, stop being a fool and go back to the College," Imer said.

"No. And if you touch me, I will resign immediately from the guard. You'll have no right to use force against the land-heir of Herun." She paused, her eyes moving from face to face. Someone sighed.

"How far do you think you'll get, with the Morgol's ship half a day behind you? She'll see you."

"Then what have you got to worry about? You know you can't let me go to Erlenstar Mountain by myself."

"Lyra. We are the chosen guard of the Morgol. We are not thieves. We are not kidnappers."

"Then go back to the College." The contempt in her voice held them motionless. "You have the choice. Go back to Herun with the Morgol. You know as much as anyone what the Star-Bearer

was. You know how he died, while the world went
about minding its own business. If no one demands
answers from the High One about the wizard who
killed him, about the shape-changers, then I think
one day much too soon a hundred guards at Crown
City will not be enough to protect the Morgol from
disaster. If I have to walk to Erlenstar Mountain,
I'll do it. Will you help me or not?"

They were silent again, lined against her, Raederle saw, like warriors in a field, their faces shadowed, unreadable. Then a small, black-haired girl
with delicate, slanting brows said resignedly, "Well,
if we can't force you to stay, maybe the ship-
master will bring you to your senses. How do you
purpose to steal his ship?"

She told them. There was grumbling, argument
over the method, but it lacked fire; their voices
died away finally. They sat waiting resignedly.
Lyra turned her horse. "All right, then."

They fell into casual position behind her. Raederle, riding beside her, saw in a wash of inn-light,
that Lyra's hands were shaking on the reins. She
frowned down at her own reins a moment, then
reached across to touch Lyra. The dark head
lifted; Lyra said, "This is the easy part, stealing a
ship."

"It's hardly stealing. It's my father's ship, and
he's in no position to quibble. I don't—there's no
one in An who will judge me, but you have your
own kind of honor."

"It's all right. It's just that I've trained for seven
years in the Morgol's guard, and in Herun I have
thirty guards under my command. It goes against
all my training to leave the Morgol like this, taking her guard with me. It's unheard of."

"She'll be safe at the College."

"I know. But what will she think of me?" She
slowed her horse as they came to the end of the

street and saw the King's ship in the moonlight, pulling restlessly at its anchor. There was a light in the charthouse. They heard a thud from the deck, and someone said, panting, "That's the last of Rood's books. If we all don't find ourselves, along with them, at the bottom of the sea, I'll eat one, iron bindings and all. I'm going for a quick cup before we sail."

Lyra glanced behind her; two of the guards dismounted, went soundlessly after him as he strode whistling down the dock. The others followed her and Raederle to the ramp of the ship. Raederle, hearing only the slough of water, the rattle of chain and her own quiet steps, glanced behind once to make sure they were still there. She felt, at their eerie silence, as though she were followed by ghosts. One slipped away at the top of the ramp to check the deck of the ship; the other two went with Lyra to the hold. Raederle waited a few moments for them to do their work beneath the deck. Then she entered the chart house, where Bri Corbett was exchanging gossip and a cup of wine with a trader. He glanced up, surprised.

"You didn't ride down alone, did you? Did Rood bring the horses up?"

"No. He's not coming."

"He's not coming? Then what does he want done with all his things?" He eyed her suspiciously. "He's not going off somewhere on his own like his father, is he?"

"No." She swallowed the dryness from her mouth. "I am. I'm going to Erlenstar Mountain; you will take me as far as Kraal. If you don't, the Morgol's ship-master, I'm sure, can be persuaded to take over the ship."

"What?" Bri Corbett rose, his grey brows lifting to his hairline. The trader was grinning. "Someone else sail your father's ship? Over my dead and buried bones, maybe. You're distraught, child, come and sit—" Lyra, spear in hand, slid like a wraith into the light, and he stopped. Raederle could hear his breathing. The trader stopped grinning. Lyra said, "Most of the crew was below. Imer and Goh have them under guard. They weren't taken seriously at first, until one man got pinned to a ladder with an arrow in his sleeve and his pant leg—he's not hurt—and Goh shot the cork out of one of the wine kegs with another. They're pleading for someone to put the cork back in."

"That's their ration of wine for the journey," Bri Corbett breathed. "Good Herun ´ wine." The trader had edged to his feet. Lyra's eyes moved to him and he stilled.

Raederle said, "Two guards followed the man who left the ship; they will be finding the rest of your crew. Bri, you wanted to go to Erlenstar Mountain anyway. You said so."

"You were—you weren't taking me seriously!"

"You might not be serious. I am."

"But your father! He'll curse the teeth out of my head when he finds out I'm taking his daughter and the land-heir of Herun on some misbegotten journey. The Morgol will have Herun up in arms."

"If you don't want to captain the ship, we'll find someone who will. There are plenty of men in the taverns, on the docks, who could be paid to take your place. If you want, we'll leave you tied somewhere along with this trader, to assure everyone of your complete innocence."

"Roust me from my own ship!" His voice cracked.

"Listen to me, Bri Corbett," she said evenly. "I lost a friend I loved and a man I might have married somewhere between Isig Pass and Erlenstar Mountain. Will you tell me what I have to go home for? More endless silence and waiting at Anuin? The Lords of the Three Portions bickering over me while the world cracks apart like Morgon's mind? Raith of Hel?"

"I know." His hand went out to her. "I understand. But you can't—"

"You said you would sail this ship to the High One's doorstep if my father had asked. Did you ever think that my father might find himself in the same danger Morgon was in? Do you want to sail comfortably back to Anuin and leave him there? If you force us by some chance off this ship, we'll go by other means. Will you want to go to Anuin and give Duac that news, on top of everything else? I have questions. I want answers to them. I am going to Erlenstar Mountain. Do you want to sail this ship for us, or shall I find someone else to do it?"

Bri Corbett brought his clenched fist down on the table. He stared at it a moment, red, wordless. Then his head lifted again slowly; he gazed at Raederle as if she had just come in the door and he had forgotten why. "You'll need another ship at Kraal. I told you that."

"I know." Her voice shook slightly at the look in his eyes.

"I can find you one at Kraal. You'll let me take it up the Winter?"

"I'd rather . . . I'd rather have you than anyone."

"We don't have supplies enough for Kraal. We'll have to stop at Caerweddin, maybe, or Hlurle."

"I've never seen Caerweddin."

"It's a beautiful city; Kraal at Isig—lovely places. I haven't seen them since . . . We'll need more wine. The crew's a good one, the best I've ever sailed with, but they worry about essentials."

"I have some money, and some jewels. I thought I might need them."

"You did." He drew a long breath. "You remind me of someone. Someone devious." The trader made an inarticulate protest, and Bri's eyes went to Lyra. "What," he inquired respectfully, "would you like to do with that one? You let him go, and he'll be pounding at the College door before we can get out of the harbor."

Lyra considered him. "We could tie him, leave him on the docks. They'll find him in the morning."

"I won't say a word," the trader said, and Bri laughed.

Raederle said quickly, "Bri, he is the one witness to the fact that you aren't responsible for this; will you remember your own reputation?"

"Lady, either I'm going because half a dozen half-grown women took over my ship, or because I'm mad enough to want to take Mathom's daughter and the Morgol's land-heir up to the high point of the world by themselves. Either way, I'm not left with much in the way of a reputation. You'd better let me see if my crew's all here; we should get underway."

They found part of the crew arriving, escorted up the ramp by two of the Morgol's guards. The men, at the sight of Bri Corbett, broke into bewildered explanations; Bri said calmly, "We're being kidnapped. You'll be getting extra pay for the privilege. We're heading north. See who is missing, and ask the rest of the men in the hold if they would kindly come up and do their jobs. Tell them to cork the wine; we'll get more in Ymris, and that they'll get no sympathy from me if they lay a finger on the Morgol's guards."

The two guards looked questioningly at Lyra, who nodded. "One of you stand at the hatch; the other watch the docks. I want this ship under guard until it clears the harbor." She added to Bri Corbett, "I trust you. But I don't know you, and I'm trained to be careful. So I'll watch you work. And remember: I've spent more nights than I can count under the open sky, and I know which stars point north."

"And I," Bri said, "have seen the Morgol's guards in training. You'll get no argument from me."

The crew appeared, disgusted and puzzled, to be dispatched to their duties under the watchful eyes of the guard. One last sailor came up the ramp singing. He eyed the guards with aplomb, winked at Lyra, and reached down to Imer, who was kneeling and tying the trader's wrists, lifted her chin in his hand and kissed her.

She pushed him away, losing her balance, and the trader, pulling the rope off his hands, caught her under the chin with his head as he rose. She sat down heavily on the deck. The trader, tripping a sailor in his way, dove for the ramp. Something he scarcely saw, glistening faintly, fell in front of him as he ran down the ramp. He ignored an arrow that cut into the wood a second before his foot hit it. The sailors crowded curiously to the rail beside the guards as they shot. Bri Corbett, shouldering between Lyra and Raederle, cursed.

"I suppose you shouldn't hit him," he said wistfully. Lyra, signalling a halt to the shooting, did not answer. There was a sudden cry and a splash; they leaned farther out over the rail. "What ails the man? Is he hurt?" They heard him cursing as he splashed in the water, then the drag of a mooring chain as he pulled himself back up. His step sounded again, quick, steady, and then there was another splash. "Madir's bones," Bri breathed. "He can't even see straight. He's coming back toward us. He must be drunk. He could tell the world I have the Morgol, the King of An and fourteen wizards aboard, for all anyone would believe his tale. Is he going in again?" There was a muffled thud. "No; he fell in a rowboat." He glanced at Raederle, who had begun to laugh weakly.

"I forgot about the water. Poor man."

Lyra's eyes slid uncertainly to her face. "What . . . Did you do something? What exactly did you do?"

She showed them her frayed cuff. "Just a little thing the pig-woman taught me to do with a tangled piece of thread . . ."

The ship got underway finally, slipping like a dream out of the dark harbor, leaving the scattering of city lights and the beacons flaring on the black horns of the land. Lyra, relaxing her guard when the ship turned unerringly northward and the west wind hit their cheeks, joined Raederle at the side. They did not speak for a while; the handful of lights vanished as the cliffs rose under the stars to block them. The jagged rim of unknown land running like a black thread against the sky was the only thing to be seen. Then Raederle, shivering a little in the cool night wind, her hands tightening on the rail, said softly, "It's what I've been wanting to do for two years, since he lost that crown somewhere around here in the bottom of the sea. But I couldn't have done it alone. I've never been farther than Caithnard in my life, and the realm seems enormous." She paused, her eyes on a moonlit swirl and dip of froth; she added with simple pain, "I only wish I had done it sooner."

Lyra's body made a rare, restive movement against the side. "How could any one of us have known to go? He was the Star-Bearer; he had a destiny. Men with destinies have their own protection. And he was travelling to the High One escorted by the High One's harpist. How could we have known that not even the High One would help him? Or help even his own harpist?"

Raederle looked at her shadowed profile. "Deth? Does the Morgol think he is dead?"

"She doesn't know. She— That was one reason she came here, to see if the Masters had any knowledge of what might have happened to him."

"Why didn't she go to Erlenstar Mountain?"

"I asked her. She said because the last landruler who had gone to see the High One was never seen nor heard of again."

Raederle was silent. Something that was not the wind sent a chill rippling through her. "I always thought Erlenstar Mountain must be the safest, the most beautiful place in the world."

"So did I." Lyra turned as the small, darkhaired guard spoke her name. "What, Kia?"

"The ship-master is giving us quarters in the king's cabin; he says it's the only one big enough for us all. Do you want a guard during the night?"

Lyra looked at Raederle. It was too dark to see her face, but Raederle could sense the question on it. She said slowly, "I would trust him. But why even tempt him to turn back? Can you stay awake?"

"In shifts." She turned to Kia again. "One guard at the helm in two hour shifts until dawn. I'll take the first watch."

"I'll join you," Raederle said.

She spent most of the two hours trying to teach Lyra the simple spell she had worked on the trader. They used a piece of twine the intrigued helmsman gave them. Lyra, frowning down at it for some minutes, threw it in the path of a sailor who walked over it and went serenely about his business.

The helmsman protested. "You'll have us all overboard," but she shook her head.

"I can't do it. I stare and stare at it, but it's only a piece of old twine. There's no magic in my blood."

"Yes, there is," Raederle said. "I felt it. In the Morgol."

Lyra looked at her curiously. "I've never felt it. One day, I'll have her power of sight. But it's a practical thing, nothing like this. This I don't understand."

"Look at it, in your mind, until it's not twine anymore but a path, looped and wound and twisted around itself, that will bind the one who touches it to its turnings . . . See it. Then put your name to it."

"How?"

"Know that you are yourself, and the thing is itself; that's the binding between you, that knowledge."

Lyra bent over the twine again. She was silent a long time, while Raederle and the helmsman watched, then Bri Corbett came out of the charthouse and Lyra tossed the twine under his boot.

"Where," he demanded of the helmsman, "in Hel's name are you taking us? Prow first into the Ymris coast?" He stepped unswervingly to the wheel and straightened their course. Lyra got to her feet with a sigh.

"I am myself, and it's an old piece of twine. That's as far as I can get. What else can you do?"

"Only a few things. Make a net out of grass, make a bramble stem seem like an impossible thorn patch, find my way out of Madir's Woods, where the trees seem to shift from place to place. . . . Little things. I inherited the powers from the wizard Madir, and someone—someone named Ylon. For some reason neither of my brothers could do such things, either. The pig-woman said magic finds its own outlet. It used to frustrate them, though, when we were children, and I could always find my way out of Madir's Woods and they never could."

"An must be a strange land. In Herun, there's very little magic, except what the wizards brought, long ago."

"In An, the land is restless with it. That's why it's such a grave thing that my father left his land indefinitely. Without his control, the magic works itself loose, and all the dead stir awake with their memories."

"What do they do?" Her voice was hushed.

"They remember old feuds, ancient hatreds, battles, and get impulses to revive them. War between the Three Portions in early times was a passionate, tumultuous thing; the old kings and lords died jealous and angry, many of them, so the land-instinct in kings grew to bind even the dead, and the spellbooks of those who played with sorcery, like Madir and Peven . . ."

"And Ylon? Who was he?"

Raederle reached down to pick up the twine. She wound it around her fingers, her brows drawn slightly as she felt the tangle run deceptively smooth and even in her hands. "A riddle."

Imer came then to relieve Lyra, and she and Raederle went gratefully to bed. The easy roll of the ship in the peaceful sea sent Raederle quickly to sleep. She woke again at dawn, before the sun rose. She dressed and went on deck. The sea, the wind, the long line of the Ymris coast were grey under the dawn sky; the mists along the vast, empty eastern horizon were beginning to whiten under the groping sunlight. The last of the guards, looking bleary at her post, glanced at the sky and headed for bed. Raederle went to the side feeling disoriented in the colorless world. She saw a tiny fishing village, a handful of houses against the bone-colored cliffs, nameless on the strange land; its minute fleet of boats was inching out of the dock into open sea. A flock of gulls wheeled crying overhead, grey and white in the morning, then scattered away southward. She wondered if they were flying to An. She felt chilly and purposeless and wondered if she had left her name behind with all her possessions at Anuin.

The sound of someone being sick over the rail made her turn. She stared mutely at the unexpected face, afraid for a moment that she had stolen out of the harbor a ship full of shape-changers. But no shape-changer, she decided, would have changed deliberately into such a miserable young girl. She waited considerately until the girl wiped her mouth and sat down in a pallid heap on the deck. Her eyes closed. Raederle, remembering Rood's agonies when he sailed, went to find the water bucket. She half-expected, returning with the dipper, that the apparition would have vanished, but it was still there, small and inconspicuous, like a bundle of old clothes in a corner.

She knelt down, and the girl lifted her head. She looked, opening her eyes, vaguely outraged, as though the sea and ship had conspired against her. Her hand shook as she took the dipper. It was a lean hand, Raederle saw, strong, brown and calloused, too big, yet, for her slender body. She emptied the dipper, leaned back against the side again.

"Thank you," she whispered. She closed her eyes. "I have never, in my entire life, felt so utterly horrible."

"It will pass. Who are you? How did you get aboard this ship?"

"I came—I came last night. I hid in one of the rowboats, under the canvas, until—until I couldn't stand it anymore. The ship was swaying one way, and the boat was swaying another. I thought I was going to die . . ." She swallowed convulsively, opened her eyes and shut them again quickly. The few freckles on her face stood out sharply. Something in the lines of her face, in the graceful determined bones of it, made Raederle's own throat close suddenly. The girl, taking a gulp of wind, continued, "I was looking for a place to stay last night when I heard you talking by the warehouses. So I just—I just followed you on board, because you were going where I want to go."

"Who are you?" Raederle whispered.

"Tristan of Hed."

Raederle sat back on her heels. A memory, brief and poignant, of Morgon's face, clearer than she had seen it for years, imposed itself over Tristan's; she felt a sharp, familiar ache in the back of her throat. Tristan looked at her with an oddly wistful expression; then turned her face quickly, huddling a little closer into her plain, shapeless cloak. She moaned as the ship lurched and said between clenched teeth, "I think I'm going to die. I heard what the Morgol's land-heir said. You stole the ship; you didn't tell anyone in your own lands. I heard the sailors talking last night, about how the guards forced them to go north, and that—that they were better off pretending they wanted to go in the first place, rather than making themselves the laughing-stock of the realm by protesting. Then they talked about the High One, and their voices went softer; I couldn't hear."

"Tristan—"

"If you put me ashore, I'll walk. You said that yourself, that you'd walk. I had to listen to Eliard crying in his sleep when he dreamed about Morgon; I would have to go wake him. He said one night—one night he saw Morgon's face in his dream, and he cou . . . he couldn't recognize him. He wanted to go then, to Erlenstar Mountain, but it was dead winter, the worst in Hed for seventy years, old Tor Oakland said, and they persuaded him to wait."

"He couldn't have gotten through the Pass."

"That's what Grim Oakland told him. He almost went anyway. But Cannon Master promised he would go, too, in spring. So spring came . . ." Her voice stopped; she sat absolutely still a moment, looking down at her hands. "Spring came and Morgon died. And all I could see in Eliard's eyes, no matter what he was doing, was one question: Why? So I'm going to Erlenstar Mountain to find out."

Raederle sighed. The sun had broken through the mists finally, patterning the deck through the criss-cross of stays with a web of light. Tristan, under its warm touch, seemed a shade less waxen; she even straightened a little without wincing. She added, "There's nothing you can say that will make me change my mind."

"It's not me, it's Bri Corbett."

"He took you and Lyra—"

"He knows me, and it's difficult to argue with the Morgol's guards. But he might balk at taking the land-heir of Hed, especially if no one knows where in the world you are. He might turn the ship around and head straight for Caithnard."

"I wrote Eliard a note. Anyway, the guards could stop him from turning."

"No. Not in open sea, when there's no one else we could get to sail the ship."

Tristan glanced painfully at the rowboat slung beside her. "I could hide again. No one's seen me."

"No. Wait." She paused, thinking. "My cabin. You could stay there. I'll bring you food."

Tristan blanched. "I don't think I'm planning to eat for a while."

"Can you walk?"

She nodded with an effort. Raederle helped her

to her feet, with a swift glance around the deck, and led her down the steps to her own small chamber. She gave Tristan a little wine, and when Tristan reeled to the bed at a sudden welter of the ship, covered her with her cloak. She lay limp, to the eye scarcely visible or breathing, but Raederle heard her voice hollow as a voice out of a barrow as she closed the door, "Thank you . . ."

She found Lyra wrapped in a dark, voluminous cloak at the stern, watching the sun rise. She greeted Raederle with a rare, impulsive smile as Raederle joined her.

Raederle said softly, so that the helmsman would not hear, "We have a problem."

"Bri?"

"No. Tristan of Hed."

Lyra stared at her incredulously. She listened silently, her brows knit, as Raederle explained. She gave a quick glance at Raederle's cabin, as though she could see through the walls to the inert form on the bed, then she said decisively, "We can't take her."

"I know."

"The people of Hed have already suffered so much over Morgon's absence; she's the land-heir of Hed, and she must be . . . How old is she?"

"Thirteen, maybe. She left them a note." She rubbed her eyes with her fingers. "If we turn back to Caithnard now, we could talk to Bri until spiders spun webs on him, and he would never agree to take us north again."

"If we turn back," Lyra said, "we may find ourselves face-to-face with the Morgol's ship. But Tristan has got to go back to Hed. Did you tell her that?"

"No. I wanted time to think. Bri said we would have to stop for supplies. We could find a tradeship to take her back."

"Would she go?"

"She isn't in any condition to argue at the moment. She's never been out of Hed in her life; I doubt if she has any idea of where Erlenstar Mountain is. She's probably never even seen a mountain in her life. But she has—she has all of Morgon's stubbornness. If we can get her off one ship and onto another while she's still seasick, then she might not realize what direction she's going until she winds up back on her own doorstep. It sounds heartless, but if she—if anything happened to her on the way to Erlenstar Mountain, I don't think anyone, in or out of Hed, could bear hearing of it. The traders will help us."

"Should we tell Bri Corbett?"

"He would turn back."

"We should turn back," Lyra said objectively, her eyes on the white scrollwork of waves on the Ymris coast. She turned her head, looked at Raederle. "It would be hard for me to face the Morgol."

"I am not going back to Anuin," Raederle said softly. "Tristan may never forgive us, but she'll have her answers, I swear by the bones of the dead of An. I swear by the name of the Star-Bearer."

Lyra's head gave a quick, pleading shake. "Don't," she breathed. "It sounds so final, as if that is the only thing you will do with your life."

Tristan slept most of the day. In the evening, Raederle brought her some hot soup; she roused herself to eat a little, then vanished back under her cloak when the night winds, coming out of the west pungent with the smell of turned earth, gave the ship an energetic roll. She moaned despairingly, but Bri Corbett, in the chart house, was pleased.

"We'll make it to Caerweddin by midmorning if this wind holds," he told Raederle when she went to bid him good-night. "It's a marvellous wind.

We'll take two hours there for supplies and still out-run anyone who might be following."

"You'd think," Raederle commented to Lyra when she went to borrow a blanket, since Tristan was sleeping on top of hers, "all this was his idea in the first place." She made herself an unsatisfying bed on the floor and woke, after a night of sketchy sleeping, feeling stiff and slightly sick herself. She stumbled into the sunlight, taking deep breaths of the mellow air, and found Bri Corbett talking to himself at the bow.

"They're not out of Kraal, they're not Ymris tradeships, too low and sleek," he murmured, leaning out over the rail. Raederle, trying to keep her hair from being whipped to a wild froth in the wind, blinked at the half-dozen ships bearing down at them. They were low, lean, single-masted ships; their billowing sails were deep blue, edged with a thin silver scallop. Bri brought one hand down on the rail with a sharp exclamation. "Madir's bones. I haven't seen one of those in ten years, not since I've been in your father's service. But I didn't hear a word of it at Caithnard."

"What?"

"War. Those are Ymris war-ships."

Raederle, suddenly awake, stared at the light, swift fleet. "They just ended a war," she protested softly to no one. "Hardly a year ago."

"We must have missed trouble by a cat's breath. It's another coastal war; they must be watching for shiploads of arms."

"Will they stop us?"

"Why should they? Do we look like a trade-ship?" He stopped then; they stared at one another, shaken by the same realization.

"No," Raederle said. "We look like the private ship of the King of An, and we're about as con-spicuous as a pig in a tree. Suppose they want to give us an escort to Caerweddin? How are you going to explain the presence of the Morgol's guards on—"

"How am I going to explain? Me? Did I hear any complaint about the color of my sails when you overran my ship and demanded I take you north?"

"How was I to know Ymris would start a war? You were the one gossiping with that trader; he didn't mention it? You didn't have to keep so close to the land; if you had kept more distance between us and Ymris, we wouldn't be running into the Ymris King's ships. Or did you know about them? Were you hoping we'd be stopped?"

"Hagis's beard!" Bri snapped indignantly. "If I wanted to turn around, there's not a guard trained yet who could stop me, especially not these—the only thing they would shoot to harm aboard this ship are knotholes and corks, I know that. I'm sailing north because I want to—and who in Hel's name is that?"

He was staring, his face a deep, veined purple, at Tristan, who had staggered out to throw up over the rail. Bri, watching, swallowed words, making little, incredulous noises in his throat. He found his voice again as Tristan straightened, mist-colored and sweating.

"Who is that?"

"She's just a—a stowaway," Raederle said futilely. "Bri, there's no need to be upset. She'll get off at Caerweddin—"

"I won't, either," Tristan said slowly but distinctly. "I'm Tristan of Hed, and I'm not getting off until we reach Erlenstar Mountain."

Bri's lips moved without sound. He seemed to billow with air like a sail; Raederle, wincing, waited to bear the brunt of it, but instead he turned and exploded across the deck to the helmsman, who jumped as if a mast had snapped behind him, "That's enough! Turn this ship around. I want her prow in the harbor at Tol so fast she leaves her reflection in the Ymris water."

The ship wheeled. Tristan clung with tight-lipped misery to the rail. Lyra, taking the last few steps to Raederle's side at a slide, saw Tristan and asked resignedly, "What happened?"

Raederle shook her head helplessly. The fierce blue of the Ymris sails came between them and the sun then; she groped for her voice. "Bri."

One of the war-ships, cutting so close she could taste the fine, sheer edge of its spray, seemed to be bearing to a single point in their path. "Bri!" She caught his attention finally as he bellowed at the sailors. "Bri! The war-ships! They think we're running from them!"

"What?" He gave the ship that was tacking to cut them off an incredulous glare and issued an order so abruptly his voice cracked. There was another lurch; the ship lost speed, slowed, and as the Ymris ship matched its pace they could see the silver mesh and sword hilts of the men aboard. Their own ship stopped and sat wallowing. Another war-ship eased to the windward side; a third guarded the stern. Bri dropped his head in his hands. A voice floated over the water; Raederle turned her head, catching only a few crisp words from a white-haired man.

Bri, shouting back an acquiescence, said briefly, heavily, "All right. Head her north again. We've got a royal escort to Caerweddin."

"Who?"

"Astrin Ymris."

65

4

THEY ENTERED THE HARBOR AT CAERWEDDIN with a war-ship at either side of them. The mouth of the river itself was guarded; there were only a few trade-ships entering, and these were stopped and searched before they were allowed farther up the broad, slow river to the docks. Raederle, Tristan, Lyra and the guards stood at the rail watching the city slide past them. Houses and shops and winding cobbled streets spilled far beyond its ancient walls and towers. The King's own house, on a rise in the center of the city, seemed a strong and forceful seat of power, with its massive blocked design and angular towers; but the carefully chosen colors in the stone made it oddly beautiful. Raederle thought of the King's house at Aniun, built to some kind of dream after the wars had ceased, of shell-white walls and high, slender towers; it would have been fragile against the forces that contended against the Ymris King. Tristan, standing beside her, reviving on the placid waters, was staring with her mouth open, and Raederle blinked away another memory of a small, quiet, oak hall, with placid, rain-drenched fields beyond it.

Lyra, frowning at the city, said softly to Raederle, as Bri Corbett gave glum orders behind them, "This is humiliating. They had no right to take us like this."

"They asked Bri if he were heading for Caerweddin; he had to say yes. He was spinning around in the water so much that he must have looked suspicious. They probably thought," she added, "when he ran, that he might have stolen the ship. Now they are probably getting ready to welcome my father to Caerweddin. They are going to be surprised."

"Where are we?" Tristan asked. It was the first word she had spoken in an hour. "Are we anywhere near Erlenstar Mountain?"

Lyra looked at her incredulously. "Haven't you even seen a map of the realm?"

"No. I never needed to."

"We are so far from Erlenstar Mountain we might as well be in Caithnard. Which is where we will be in two days' time anyway—"

"No," Raederle said abruptly. "I'm not going back."

"I'm not either," Tristan said. Lyra met Raederle's eyes above her head.

"All right. But do you have any suggestions?"

"I'm thinking."

The ship docked alongside of one of the warships; the other, waiting, in a gesture at once courteous and prudent, until Bri sank anchor into the deep water, then turned and made its way back toward the sea. The splash of iron, the long rattle and thump of the anchor chain sounded in the air like the final word of an argument. They saw, as the ramp slid down, a small group of men arrive on horseback, richly dressed and armed. Bri Corbett went down to meet them. A man in blue livery carried a blue and silver banner. Raederle, realizing what it was, felt the blood pound suddenly into her face.

"One of them must be the King," she whispered, and Tristan gave her an appalled look.

"I'm not going down there. Look at my skirt."

"Tristan, you are the land-heir of Hed, and once they learn that, we could be dressed in leaves and berries for all they'll realize what we're wearing."

"Should we carry our spears down?" Imer asked puzzledly. "We would if the Morgol were with us."

Lyra considered the matter blankly. Her mouth crooked a little. "I believe I have deserted. A spear in the hand of a dishonored guard isn't an emblem but a challenge. However, since this is my responsibility, you're free to make your own decision."

Imer sighed. "You know, we could have locked you in the cabin and told Bri Corbett to turn around. We talked about it that first night, when you took the watch. That was one mistake you made. We made our own decision, then."

"Imer, it's different for me! The Morgol will have to forgive me eventually, but what will all of you go home to?"

"If we do get home, bringing you with us," Imer said calmly, "the Morgol will probably be a lot more reasonable than you are. I think she would rather have us with you than not. The King," she added a little nervously, looking over Lyra's shoulder, "is coming on board."

Raederle, turning to face him, felt Tristan grip her wrist. The King looked formidable at first glance, dark, powerful and grim, with body armor like the delicate, silvery scales of fish, beneath a blue-black surcoat whorled with endless silver embroidery. The white-haired man of the war-ship came with him, with his single white eye; his other eye was sealed shut against something he had seen.

As they stood together, she felt the binding between them, like the binding between Duac and Mathom, and recognized, with a slight shock, the eccentric land-heir of the Ymris King. His good eye went suddenly to her face, as though he had sensed her recognition. The King surveyed them silently a moment. Then he said with simple, unexpected kindliness, "I am Heureu Ymris. This is my land-heir, my brother Astrin. Your ship-master told me who you are, and that you are travelling together under peculiar circumstances. He requested a guard for you past the Ymris coast, since we are at war, and he wanted no harm to come to such valuable passengers. I have seven war-ships preparing to leave at dawn for Meremont. They will give you an escort south. Meanwhile, you are very welcome to my land and my house."

He paused, waiting. Lyra said abruptly, a slight flush on her face, "Did Bri Corbett tell you that we took his ship? That we—that I—that none of the Morgol's guard are acting with her knowledge? I want you to understand who you will welcome into your house."

There was a flick of surprise in his eyes, followed by another kind of recognition. He said gently, "Don't you think you were trying to do exactly what many of us this past year have only thought of doing? You will honor my house."

They followed him and his land-heir down the ramp; he introduced them to the High Lords of Marcher and Tor, the red-haired High Lord of Umber, while their horses were unloaded. They mounted, made a weary, slightly bedraggled procession behind the King. Lyra, riding abreast of Raederle, her eyes on Heureu Ymris's back, whispered, "Seven war-ships. He's taking no chances with us. What if you threw a piece of gold thread in the water in front of them?"

"I'm thinking," Raederle murmured.

In the King's house, they were given small, light, richly furnished chambers where they could wash and rest in private. Raederle, concerned for Tristan in the great, strange house, watched her ignore servants and riches, and crawl thankfully into a bed that did not move. In her own chamber, she washed the sea spray out of her hair, and, feeling clean for the first time in days, stood by the open window combing her hair dry and looking out over the unfamiliar land. Her eyes wandered down past the busy maze of streets, picked out the old city wall, broken here and there by gates and arches above the streets. The city scattered eventually into farmland and forest, orchards that were soft mists of color in the distance. Then, her eyes moving east again to the sea, she saw something that made her put her comb down, lean out the open casement.

There was a stonework, enormous and puzzling, on a cliff not far from the city. It stood like some half-forgotten memory, or the fragments on a torn page of ancient, incomplete riddles. The stones she recognized, beautiful, massive, vivid with color. The structure itself, bigger than anything any man would have needed, had been shaken to the ground seemingly with as much ease as she would have shaken ripe apples out of a tree. She swallowed drily, remembering tales her father had made her learn, remembering something Morgon had mentioned briefly in one of his letters, remembering, above all, the news Elieu had brought from Isig about the waking, in the soundless deep of the Mountain, of the children of the Earth-Masters. Then something beyond all comprehension, a longing, a loneliness, an understanding played in the dark rim of her mind, bewildering her with its sorrow and recognition, frightening her with its intensity, until she could neither bear to look at the nameless city, nor turn away from it.

A knock sounded softly at her door; she realized then that she was standing blind, with tears running down her face. The world, with a physical effort, as if two great stones locked massively, ponderously into position, shifted back into familiarity. The knock came again; she wiped her face with the back of her hand and went to open it.

The Ymris land-heir, standing in the doorway, with his alien face and single white eye startled her for some reason. Then she saw its youngness, the lines worn in it of pain and patience. He said quickly, gently, "What is it? I came to talk with you a little, about the—about Morgon. I can come back."

She shook her head. "No. Please come in. I was just—I—" She stopped helplessly, wondering if he could understand the words she had to use. Some instinct made her reach out to him, grip him as though to keep her balance; she said, half-blind again, "People used to say you lived among the ruins of another time, that you knew unearthly things. There are things—there are things I need to ask."

He stepped into the room, closed the door behind him. "Sit down," he said, and she sat in one of the chairs by the cold hearth. He brought her a cup of wine, then took a chair beside her. He looked, still wearing mail and the King's dark livery of war, like a warrior, but the slight perplexity in his face was of no such simple mind.

"You have power," he said abruptly. "Did you know that?"

"I know—I have a little. But now, I think, there may be things in me I never—I never knew." She took a swallow of wine; her voice grew calmer. "Do you know the riddle of Oen and Ylon?"

"Yes." Something moved in his good eye. He said, "Yes," again, softly. "Ylon was a shape-changer."

She moved slightly, as away from a pain. "His blood runs in the family of the Kings of An. For centuries he was little more than a sad tale. But now, I want—I have to know. He came out of the sea, like the shape-changer Lyra saw, the one who nearly killed Morgon—he was of that color and wildness. Whatever—whatever power I have comes from Madir. And from Ylon."

He was silent for a long time, contemplating the riddle she had given him while she sipped wine, the cup in her hands shaking slightly. He said finally, groping, "What made you cry?"

"That dead city. It—something in me reached out and knew . . . and knew what it had been."

His good eye moved to her face; his voice caught. "What was it?"

"I was—I stood in the way. It was like someone else's memory in me. It frightened me. I thought, when I saw you, that you might understand."

"I don't understand either you or Morgon. Maybe you, like him, are an integral piece in some great puzzle as old and complex as that city on King's Mouth Plain. All I know of the cities is the broken things I find, hardly a trace of the Earth-Masters' passage. Morgon had to grope for his own power, as you will; what he is now, after—"

"Wait." Her voice shook again, uncontrollably. "Wait."

He leaned forward, took the unsteady cup from her and set it on the floor. Then he took her hands in his own lean, tense hands. "Surely you don't believe he is dead."

"Well, what alternative do I have? What's the dark side to that tossed coin—whether he's alive or dead, whether he's dead or his mind is broken under that terrible power—"

"Who broke whose power? For the first time in seven centuries the wizards are freed—"

"Because the Star-Bearer is dead! Because the one who killed him no longer needs to fear their power."

"Do you believe that? That's what Heureu says, and Rork Umber. The wizard Aloil had been a tree on King's Mouth Plain for seven centuries, until I watched him turn into himself, bewildered with his freedom. He spoke only briefly to me; he didn't know why he had been freed; he had never heard of the Star-Bearer. He had dead white hair and eyes that had watched his own destruction. I asked where he would go, and he only laughed and vanished. Then, a few days later, traders brought the terrible tale out of Hed of Morgon's torment, of the passing of the land-rule, on the day Aloil had been freed. I have never believed that Morgon is dead."

"What . . . Then what is left of him? He has lost everything he loved, he has lost his own name. When Awn—when Awn of An lost his own land-rule while he was living, he killed himself. He couldn't—"

"I lived with Morgon when he was nameless once before. He found his name again in the stars that he bears. I will not believe he is dead."

"Why?"

"Because that isn't the answer he was looking for."

She stared at him incredulously. "You don't think he had a choice in the matter?"

"No. He is the Star-Bearer. I think he was destined to live."

"You make that sound more like a doom," she whispered. He loosed her hands and rose, went to stand at the window where she had been gazing out at the nameless city.

"Perhaps. But I would never underestimate that farmer from Hed." He turned suddenly. "Will you ride with me to King's Mouth Plain, to see the ancient city?"

"Now? I thought you had a war to fight."

His unexpected smile warmed his lean face. "I did, until we saw your ship. You gave me a respite until dawn, when I lead you and your escort out of Caerweddin. It's not a safe place, that plain. Heureu's wife was killed there. No one goes there now but me, and even I am wary. But you might find something—a stone, a broken artifact—that will speak to you."

She rode with him through Caerweddin, up the steep, rocky slope onto the plain above the sea. The sea winds sang hollowly across it, trailing between the huge, still stones that had rooted deep into the earth through countless centuries. Raederle, dismounting, laid her hand on one impulsively; it was clear, smooth under her palm, shot through with veins of emerald green.

"It's so beautiful. . . ." She looked at Astrin suddenly. "That's where the stones of your house came from."

"Yes. Whatever pattern these stones made has been hopelessly disturbed. The stones were nearly impossible to move, but the King who took them, Galil Ymris, was a persistent man." He bent down abruptly, searched the long grass and earth in the crook of two stones and rose again with something in his hand. He brushed it off: it winked star-blue in the sunlight. She looked at it as it lay in his palm.

"What is it?"

"I don't know. A piece of cut glass, a stone. . . . It's hard to tell sometimes exactly what things are here." He dropped it into her own hand, closed her fingers around it lightly. "You keep it."

She turned it curiously, watched it sparkle. "You love these great stones, in spite of all their danger."

"Yes. That makes me strange, in Ymris. I would rather putter among forgotten things like an old hermit-scholar than take seven war-ships into battle. But war on the south coasts is an old sore that festers constantly and never seems to heal. So Heureu needs me there, even though I try to tell him I can taste and smell and feel some vital answer in this place. And you. What do you feel from it?"

She lifted her eyes from the small stone, looked down the long scattering of stones. The plain was empty but for the stones, the silver-edged grass and a single stand of oak, gnarled and twisted by the sea wind. The cloudless sky curved away from it, building to an immensity of nothingness. She wondered what force could ever draw the stones again up into it, straining out of the ground, pulled one onto another, building to some immense, half-comprehensible purpose that would shine from a distance with power, beauty and a freedom like the wind's freedom. But they lay still, gripped to the earth, dormant. She whispered, "Silence," and the wind died.

She felt, in that moment, as if the world had stopped. The grass was motionless in the sunlight; the shadows of the stones seemed measured and blocked on the ground. Even the breakers booming at the cliff's foot were still. Her own breath lay indrawn in her mouth. Then Astrin touched her, and she heard the unexpected hiss of his sword from the scabbard. He pulled her against him, holding her tightly. She felt, under the cold mesh of armor, the hard pound of his heart.

There was a sigh out of the core of the world.

A wave that seemed as if it would never stop gathering shook the cliff as it broke and withdrew. Astrin's arm dropped. She saw his face as she stepped back; the drawn, hollow look frightened her. A gull cried, hovering at the cliff's edge, then disappeared; she saw him shudder. He said briefly, "I'm terrified. I can't think. Let's go."

They were both silent as they rode down the slope again towards the lower fields and the busy north road into the city. As they cut across a field full of sheep bawling with the indignity of being shorn, the white, private horror eased away from Astrin's face. Raederle, glancing at him, felt him accessible again; she said softly, "What was it? Everything seemed to stop."

"I don't know. The last time—the last time I felt it, Eriel Ymris died. I was afraid for you."

"Me?"

"For five years after she died, the King lived with a shape-changer as his wife."

Raederle closed her eyes. She felt something build in her suddenly, like a shout she wanted to loose at him that would drown even the voices of the sheep. She clenched her hands, controlling it; she did not realize she had stopped until he spoke her name. Then she opened her eyes and said, "At least he had no land-heir to lock away in a tower by the sea. Astrin, I think there is something sleeping inside of me, and if I wake it, I will regret it until the world's end. I have a shape-changer's blood in me, and something of his power. That's an awkward thing to have."

His good eye, quiet again, seemed to probe with detachment to the heart of her riddle. "Trust yourself," he suggested, and she drew a deep breath.

"That's like stepping with my eyes shut onto one of my own tangled threads. You have a comforting outlook on things."

He gripped her wrist lightly before they started to ride again. She found, her hand easing open, the mark of the small stone she held ridged deeply into her palm.

Lyra came to talk to her when she returned to the King's house. Raederle was sitting at the window, looking down at something that sparkled like a drop of water in her hand. "Have you thought of a plan yet?" Lyra said.

Raederle, lifting her head, sensed the restlessness and frustration in her tight, controlled movements, like the movements of some animal trapped and tempered into civility. She gathered her thoughts with an effort.

"I think Bri Corbett could be persuaded to turn us north after we leave the river, if we can get Tristan on her way home. But Lyra, I don't know what would persuade Astrin Ymris to let us go."

"The decision is ours; it has nothing to do with Ymris."

"It would be hard to convince either Astrin or Heureu of that."

Lyra turned abruptly away from the window, paced to the empty grate and back. "We could find another ship. No. They'd only search us, going out of the harbor." She looked as close as she would ever come to throwing something that was not a weapon. Then, glancing down at Raederle, she said unexpectedly, "What's the matter? You look troubled."

"I am," Raederle said, surprised. Her head bent; her hand closed again over the stone. "Astrin— Astrin told me he thinks Morgon is alive."

She heard a word catch in Lyra's throat. Lyra sat down suddenly next to her, gripping the stone ledge with her hands. Her face was white; she found her voice again, pleaded, "What—what makes him think so?"

"He said Morgon was looking for answers, and death wasn't one of them. He said—"

"That would mean he lost the land-rule. That was his greatest fear. But no one—no one can take away that instinct but the High One. No one—" She stopped. Raederle heard the sudden clench of her teeth. She leaned back wearily, the stone shining like a tear in her palm. Lyra's voice came again, unfamiliar, stripped bare of all passion, "I will kill him for that."

"Who?"

"Ghisteslwchlohm."

Raederle's lips parted and closed. She waited for the chill that the strange voice had roused in her to subside, then she said carefully, "You'll have to find him first. That may be difficult."

"I'll find him. Morgon will know where he is."

"Lyra—" Lyra's face turned toward her, and the words of prudence caught in Raederle's throat. She looked down. "First we have to get out of Caerweddin."

The dark, unfamiliar thing eased out of Lyra. She said anxiously, "Don't tell Tristan what you told me. It's too uncertain."

"I won't."

"Isn't there something you can do for us? We can't turn back now. Not now. Make a wind blow the war-ships away, make them see an illusion of us going south—"

"What do you think I am? A wizard? I don't think even Madir could do those things." A bead of sunlight caught in the strange stone; she straightened suddenly. "Wait." She held it up between forefinger and thumb, catching the sun's rays. Lyra blinked as the light slid over her eyes.

"What? What is that?"

"It's a stone Astrin found on King's Mouth Plain, in the city of the Earth-Masters. He gave it to me."

78

"What are you going to do with it?" Her eyes narrowed again as the bright light touched them, and Raederle lowered it.

"It flashes like a mirror . . . All I learned from the pig-woman is concerned with illusion, small things out of proportion: the handful of water seeming a pool, the twig a great fallen log, the single bramble stem an impassible tangle. If I could —if I could blind the war-ships with this, make it blaze like a sun in their eyes, they couldn't see us turn north, they wouldn't be able to outrun us."

"With that? It's no bigger than a thumbnail. Besides," she added uneasily, "how do you know what it is? You know a handful of water is a handful of water. But you don't know what this was meant for, so how will you know exactly what it might become?"

"If you don't want me to try it, I won't. It's a decision that will affect us all. It's also the only thing I can think of."

"You're the one who has to work with it. How do you know what name the Earth-Masters might have put to it? I'm not afraid for us or the ship, but it's your mind—"

"Did I," Raederle interrupted, "offer you advice?"

"No," Lyra said reluctantly. "But I know what I'm doing."

"Yes. You're going to get killed by a wizard. Am I arguing?"

"No. But—" She sighed. "All right. Now all we have to do is tell Bri Corbett where he's going so that he'll know to get supplies. And we have to send Tristan home. Can you think of any possible way to do that?"

They both thought. An hour later, Lyra slipped unostensibly out of the King's house, went down to the docks to inform Bri that he was heading north again, and Raederle went to the King's hall to talk to Heureu Ymris.

She found him in the midst of his lords, discussing the situation in Meremont. When he saw her hesitating at the doorway of the great hall, he came to her. Meeting his clear, direct gaze, she knew that she and Lyra had been right: he would be less difficult to deceive than Astrin, and she was relieved that Astrin was not with him. He said, "Is there something you need? Something I can help you with?"

She nodded. "Could I talk to you a moment?"

"Of course."

"Could you—is it possible for you to spare one of your war-ships to take Tristan home? Bri Corbett will have to stop at Caithnard to let Lyra off and pick up my brother. Tristan is unreasonably determined to get to Erlenstar Mountain, and if she can find a way to get off Bri's ship at Caithnard, she'll do it. She'll head north, either on a tradeship or on foot, and either way she is liable to find herself in the middle of your war."

His dark brows knit. "She sounds stubborn. Like Morgon."

"Yes. And if she—if anything happened to her, too, it would be devastating to the people of Hed. Bri could take her to Hed before he brings us to Caithnard, but in those waters he must pass over, Athol and Spring of Hed were drowned, and Morgon was nearly killed. I would feel easier if she had a little more protection than a few guards and sailors."

He drew a quick, silent breath. "I hadn't thought of that. Only five of the war-ships are carrying a great many arms and men; two are more lightly manned patrols watching for shiploads of arms. I can spare one to take her back. If I could, I would send those war-ships with you all the way to

Caithnard. I have never seen such a valuable assortment of people on such a misguided, ill-considered journey in my life."

She flushed a little. "I know. It was wrong of us to take Tristan even this far."

"Tristan! What about you and the Morgol's land-heir?"

"That's different—"

"How, in Yrth's name?"

"We at least know there's a world between Hed and the High One."

"Yes," he said grimly. "And it's no place for any of you, these days. I made sure your ship-master understood that, too. I don't know what possessed him to leave the Caithnard harbor with you."

"It wasn't his fault. We didn't give him any choice."

"How much duress could you possibly have put him under? The Morgol's guards are skilled, but hardly unreasonable. And you might as easily have met worse than my war-ships off the Ymris coast. There are times when I believe I am fighting only my own rebels, but at other times, the entire war seems to change shape under my eyes, and I realize that I am not even sure myself how far it will extend, or if I can contain it. Small as it is yet, it has terrifying potential. Bri Corbett could not have chosen a worse time to sail with you so close to Meremont."

"He didn't know about the war—"

"If he had been carrying your father on that ship, he would have made it his business to know. I reminded him of that, also. As for Astrin taking you today to King's Mouth Plain—that was utter stupidity." He stopped. She saw the light glance white off his cheekbones before he lifted his hands to his eyes, held them there a moment. She looked down, swallowing.

"I suppose you told him that."

"Yes. He seemed to agree with me. This is no time for people of intelligence, like Astrin, you and Bri Corbett, to forget how to think." He put a hand on her shoulder then, and his voice softened. "I understand what you were trying to do. I understand why. But leave it for those who are more capable."

She checked an answer and bent her head, yielding him tacitly the last word. She said with real gratitude, "Thank you for the ship. Will you tell Tristan in the morning?"

"I'll escort her personally on board."

Raederle saw Lyra again later in the hall as they were going to supper. Lyra said softly, "Bri argued, but I swore to him on what's left of my honor that he would not have to try to outrun the war-ships. He didn't like it, but he remembered what you did with that piece of thread. He said whatever you do tomorrow had better be effective, because he won't dare face Heureu Ymris again if it isn't."

Raederle felt her face burn slightly at a memory. "Neither will I," she murmured. Tristan came out of her room then, bewildered and a little frightened, as if she had just wakened. Her face eased at the sight of them; at the trust in her eyes, Raederle felt a pang of guilt. She said, "Are you hungry? We're going down to the King's hall to eat."

"In front of people?" She brushed hopelessly at her wrinkled skirt. Then she stopped, looked around her at the beautifully patterned walls glistening with torchlight, the old shields of bronze and silver hung on them, the ancient, jeweled weapons. She whispered, "Morgon was in this house," and her shoulders straightened as she followed them to the hall.

THEY WERE WAKENED BEFORE DAWN THE NEXT morning. Bundled in rich, warm cloaks Heureu gave them, they rode with him, Astrin, the High Lords of Umber and Tor and three hundred armed men through the quiet streets of Caerweddin. They saw windows opening here and there, or the spill of light from a door as a face peered out at the quick, silent march of warriors. At the docks, the dark masts loomed out of a pearl-colored mist over the water; the voices, the footsteps in the dawn seemed muted, disembodied. The men broke out of their lines, began to board. Bri Corbett, coming down the ramp, gave Raederle one grim, harassed glance before he took her horse up. The Morgol's guards followed him up with their horses.

Raederle waited a moment, to hear Heureu say to Tristan, "I'm sending you home with Astrin in one of the warships. You'll be safe with him, well-protected by the men with him. It's a fast ship; you'll be home quickly."

Raederle, watching, could not tell for a moment who looked more surprised, Tristan or Astrin. Then Tristan, her mouth opening to protest, saw Raederle listening and an indignant realization leaped into her eyes. Astrin said before she could speak, "That's over two days there and a day back to Meremont—you'll need that ship to watch the coast."

"I can spare it that long. If the rebels have sent for arms, they'll come down most likely from the north, and I can try to stop them at Caerweddin."

"Arms," Astrin argued, "are not all we're watching for." Then his eyes moved slowly from Heureu's face to Raederle's. "Who requested that ship?"

"I made the decision," Heureu said crisply, and at his tone, Tristan, who had opened her mouth again, closed it abruptly.

Astrin gazed at Raederle, his brows puckered in suspicion and perplexity. He said briefly to Heureu,

"All right. I'll send you word from Meremont when I return."

"Thank you." His fingers closed a moment on Astrin's arm. "Be careful."

Raederle boarded. She went to the stern, heard Bri's voice giving oddly colorless orders behind her. The first of the war-ships began to drift like some dark bird to the middle of the river; as it moved the mist began to swirl and fray over the quiet grey water, and the first sunlight broke on the high walls of the King's house.

Lyra came to stand beside Raederle. Neither of them spoke. The ship bearing Tristan slid alongside them, and Raederle saw Astrin's face, with its spare lines and ghostly coloring, as he watched the rest of the war-ships ease into position behind him. Bri Corbett, with his slower, heavier vessel, went last, in the wake of the staggered line. In their own wake came the sun.

It burned the froth behind them. Bri said softly to the helmsman, "Be ready to turn her at half a word. If those ships slow and close around us in open sea, we might as well take off our boots and wade to Kraal. And that's what I intend to do if they give chase and stop us. Astrin Ymris would singe one ear off me with his tongue and Heureu the other, and I could carry what's left of my reputation back to Anuin with me in a boot with a hole in it."

"Don't worry," Raederle murmured. The stone flashed like a king's jewel in her hand. "Bri, I'll need to float this behind us or it will blind us all. Do you have a piece of wood or something?"

"I'll find one." The placid sigh of the morning tide caught their ears; he turned his head. The first ship was already slipping into the open sea. He said again, nervously as the salt wind teased at their sails, "I'll find one. You do whatever it is you're doing."

Raederle bent her head, looked down at the stone. It dazzled like a piece of sun-shot ice, light leaping from plane to plane of its intricately cut sides. She wondered what it had been, saw it in her mind's eye as a jewel in a ring, the center eye of a crown, the pommel of a knife, perhaps, that darkened in times of danger. But did the Earth-Masters ever use such things? Had it belonged to them or to some fine lady in the Ymris court who dropped it as she rode or to some trader who bought it in Isig, then lost it, flickering out of his pack as he crossed King's Mouth Plain? If it could blaze like a tiny star in her hand at the sun's touch, she knew the illusion of it would ignite the sea, and no ship would see to pass through it, even if it dared. But what was it?

The light played gently in her mind, dispersing old night-shadows, pettinesses, the little, nagging memories of dreams. Her thoughts strayed to the great plain where it had been found, the massive stones on it like monuments to a field of ancient dead. She saw the morning sunlight sparkle in the veins of color on one stone, gather in a tiny fleck of silver in a corner of it. She watched that minute light in her mind, kindled it slowly with the sunlight caught in the stone she held. It began to glow softly in her palm. She fed the light in her mind; it spilled across the ageless stones, dispersing their shadows; she felt the warmth of the light in her hand, on her face. The light began to engulf the stones in her mind, arch across the clear sky until it dazzled white; she heard as from another time, a soft exclamation from Bri Corbett. The twin lights drew from one another: the light in her hand, the light in her mind. There was a flurry of words, cries, faint and meaningless behind her.

The ship reeled, jolting her; she reached out to catch her balance, and the light at her face burned her eyes.

"All right," Bri said breathlessly. "All right. You've got it. Put it down—it'll float on this." His own eyes were nearly shut, wincing against it.

She let him guide her hand, heard the stone clink into the small wooden bowl he held. Sailors let it over the side in a net as if they were lowering the sun into the sea. The gentle waves danced it away. She followed it with her mind, watching the white light shape into facet after facet in her mind, harden with lines and surfaces, until her whole mind seemed a single jewel, and looking into it, she began to sense its purpose.

She saw someone stand, as she stood, holding the jewel. He was in the middle of a plain in some land, in some age, and as the stone winked in his palm all movement around him, beyond the rim of her mind, began to flow towards its center. She had never seen him before, but she felt suddenly that his next gesture, a line of bone in his face if he turned, would give her his name. She waited curiously for that moment, watching him as he watched the stone, lost in the timeless moment of his existence. And then she felt a stranger's mind in her own, waiting with her.

Its curiosity was desperate, dangerous. She tried to pull away from it, frightened, but the startling, unfamiliar awareness of someone else's mind would not leave her. She sensed its attention on the nameless stranger whose next movement, the bend of his head, the spread of his fingers, would give her his identity. A terror, helpless and irrational, grew in her at the thought of that recognition, of yielding whatever name he held to the dark, powerful mind bent on discovering it. She struggled to disperse the image in her mind before he moved.

But the strange power held her; she could neither change the image nor dispel it, as though her mind's eye were gazing, lidless, into the core of an incomprehensible mystery. Then a hand whipped, swift, hard, across her face; she pulled back, flinching against a strong grip.

The ship, scudding in the wind, boomed across a wave, and she blinked the spray out of her eyes. Lyra, holding her tightly, whispered, "I'm sorry. I'm sorry. But you were screaming." The light had gone; the King's war-ships were circling one another bewilderedly far behind them. Bri, his face colorless as he looked at her, breathed, "Shall I take you back? Say the word, and I'll turn back."

"No. It's all right." Lyra loosed her slowly; Raederle said again, the back of her hand over her mouth, "It's all right, now, Bri."

"What was it?" Lyra said. "What was that stone?"

"I don't know." She felt the aftermath of the strange mind again, demanding, insistent; she shuddered. "I almost knew something—"

"What?"

"I don't know! Something important to someone. But I don't know what, I don't know why—" She shook her head hopelessly. "It was like a dream, so important then, and now it's—it makes no sense. All I know is that there were twelve."

"Twelve what?"

"Twelve sides to that stone. Like a compass." She saw Bri Corbett's bewildered expression. "I know. It makes no sense."

"But what in Hel's name made you scream like that?" he demanded.

She remembered the powerful, relentless mind that had trapped her own in its curiosity, and knew that though he would turn back to face even the war-ships again if she told him of it, there would be no place in the realm where she could be truly safe from it. She said softly, "It was something of power, that stone. I should have used a simpler thing. I'm going to rest awhile."

She did not come out of her cabin again until evening. She went to the side, then, stood watching stars burn like distant reflections of her mind-work. Something made her turn her head suddenly. She saw, swaying comfortably to the ship's motion, Tristan of Hed, standing like a figurehead at the prow.

5

TRISTAN WOULD NOT SPEAK TO ANYONE FOR TWO days. Bri Corbett, torn between taking her back and avoiding at all costs the hoodwinked escort and the one-eyed Ymris prince, spent a day cursing, then yielded to Tristan's mute, reproachful determination and sailed north on his own indecision. They left, at the end of those two days, the Ymris coastline behind them. The unsettled forests, the long stretch of barren hills between Herun and the sea were all they saw for a while, and gradually they began to relax. The wind was brisk; Bri Corbett, his face cheerful and ruddy under the constant sun, kept the sailors jumping. The guards, unused to idleness, practiced knife throwing at a target on the wall of the chart house. When a sudden roll of the ship caused a wild throw that nearly sliced a cable in two, Bri put a halt to that. They took up fishing instead, with long lines trailing from the stern. Sailors, watching as they bent over the rail, remembered the dead thwick of knife blade into the chart house wall and approached with caution.

Raederle, after futile attempts to soothe Tristan,

who stood aloof and quiet, looking northward like a dark reminder of their purpose, gave up and left her alone. She stayed quiet herself, reading Rood's books or playing the flute she had brought from Anuin, that Elieu of Hel had made for her. One afternoon she sat on the deck with it and played songs and court dances of An and plaintive ballads that Cyone had taught her years before. She wandered into a sad, simple air she could not recall the name of and found, when she finished, that Tristan had turned away from the rail and was watching her.

"That was from Hed," she said abruptly. Raederle rested the flute on her knees, remembering.

"Deth taught it to me."

Tristan, wavering, moved away from the rail finally, sat down beside her on the warm deck. Her face was expressionless; she did not speak.

Raederle, her eyes on the flute, said softly, "Please try to understand. When the news of Morgon's death came, it was not only Hed that suffered a loss, but people all over the realm who had helped him, who loved him and worried about him. Lyra and Bri and I were simply trying to spare the realm, your own people especially, more fear and worry about you. Hed seems a very special and vulnerable place these days. We didn't mean to hurt you, but we didn't want, if anything had happened to you, to be hurt again ourselves."

Tristan was silent. She lifted her head slowly, leaned back against the side. "Nothing's going to happen to me." She looked at Raederle a moment, asked a little shyly, "Would you have married Morgon?"

Raederle's mouth crooked. "I waited two years for him to come to Anuin and ask me."

"I wish he had. He never was very sensible." She gathered her knees up, rested her chin on them, brooding. "I heard the traders say he could change shape into an animal. That frightened Eliard. Can you do that?"

"Change shape? No." Her hands tightened slightly on the flute. "No."

"And then they said—they said last spring he had found a starred sword and killed with it. That didn't sound like him."

"No."

"But Grim Oakland said if someone were trying to kill him, he couldn't just stand there and let them. I can understand that; it's reasonable, but . . . after that, with someone else making a harp and a sword for him that were his because of the stars on his face, he didn't seem to belong to Hed any more. It seemed he couldn't come back and do the simple things he had always done—feed the pigs, argue with Eliard, make beer in the cellar. It seemed he had already left us forever, because we didn't really know him any more."

"I know," Raederle whispered. "I felt that way, too."

"So—in that way—it wasn't so hard when he died. What was hard was knowing . . . was knowing what he was going through before he died and not being able to—not—" Her voice shook; she pressed her mouth tightly against one arm. Raederle tilted her head back against the side, her eyes on the shadow the boom cut across the deck.

"Tristan. In An, the passage of the land-rule is a complex and startling thing, they say, like suddenly growing an extra eye to see in the dark or an ear to hear things beneath the earth . . . Is it that way in Hed?"

"It didn't seem that way." Her voice steadied as she mulled over the question. "Eliard was out in the fields when it happened. He just said he felt that suddenly everything—the leaves and animals, the rivers, the seedlings—everything suddenly made sense. He knew what they were and why they did what they did. He tried to explain it to me. I said everything must have made sense before, most things do anyway, but he said it was different. He could see everything very clearly, and what he couldn't see he felt. He couldn't explain it very well."

"Did he feel Morgon die?"

"No. He—" Her voice stopped. Her hands shifted, tightened on her knees; she went on in a whisper, "Eliard said Morgon must have forgotten even who he was when he died, because of that."

Raederle winced. She put her hand on Tristan's taut arm. "I'm sorry. I wasn't trying to be cruel; I was just—"

"Curious. Like Morgon."

"No!" The pain in her own voice made Tristan lift her head, look at her surprisedly.

She was silent again, studying Raederle almost as though she had never seen her before. She said, "There's something I've always wondered, in the back of my mind, from the first time I heard about you."

"What?"

"Who is the most beautiful woman in An?" She flushed a little at Raederle's sudden smile, but there was a shy, answering smile in her eyes. "I was always curious."

"The most beautiful woman in An is Map Hwillion's sister, Mara, who married the lord Cyn Croeg of Aum. She is called the Flower of An."

"What are you called?"

"Just the second most beautiful woman."

"I've never seen anyone more beautiful than you. When Morgon first told us about you, I was frightened. I didn't think you could live in Hed, in

our house. But now . . . I don't know. I wish—
I wish things had turned out differently."

"So do I," Raederle said softly. "And now, will
you tell me something? How in the world did you
manage to get off that war-ship and onto this one
without anyone, Astrin, Heureu, Bri or all those
warriors seeing you?"

Tristan smiled. "I just followed the King onto
the war-ship and then followed him off again. Nobody expected to see me where I wasn't supposed
to be, and so they didn't. It was simple."

They passed Hlurle at night. Bri Corbett, with
thought of another cask of Herun wine, suggested
a brief stop there until Lyra reminded him of the
twenty guards waiting at Hurle to escort the
Morgol back to Herun. He abandoned the idea
hastily and stopped instead farther up the coast, at
the mouth of the turbulent Ose, where they took a
quick, welcome respite from the sea. The town
there was small, full of fishermen and trappers
who brought their furs twice a year from the wil-
derness to sell to the traders. Bri bought wine, all
the fresh eggs he could find and replenished their
water supply. Lyra, Raederle and Tristan left letters for the traders to take south. No one recognized them, but they departed in a wake of
curiosity that the letters, astonishingly addressed,
did nothing to abate.

Three days later, at midmorning, they reached
Kraal.

The city straddling Winter River was rough-
hewn out of the stones and timber of Osterland.
Beyond it, they caught their first close glimpse of
the wild land, shaggy with pine, and of the distant
blue-white mist of mountains. The harbor was full
of trade-ships, barges with their gleaming upright
lines of oars, riverboats making their slow way up
the deep, green waters.

Bri, maneuvering carefully through the crowd, seemed to be calculating every shiver of wood under his feet, every wrinkle that appeared in the sails. He took the wheel from the helmsman once; Raederle heard him say, "That current must be dragging the barnacles off the hull. I've never seen the water so high. It must have been a terrible winter through the Pass . . ."

He found a berth unexpectedly in the crowded docks; the sight of the blue and purple sails of the King of An and the ship's incongruous passengers caused brisk and audible speculation among the shrewd-eyed traders. The women were all recognized as they stood at the rails, before the ship was fully secured to the moorings. Tristan's mouth dropped as she heard her own name, coupled with an unflattering query of the state of Bri Corbett's mind, shouted across the water from a neighboring ship.

Bri ignored it, but the burn on his face seemed to deepen. He said to Raederle as the ramp slid down, "You'll get no peace in this city, but at least you've got a good escort if you want to leave the ship. I'll try to get a barge and oarsmen; it'll be slow, and it will cost. But if we wait for the snow water to abate and a halfway decent wind to sail up, we may find the Morgol herself joining us. And that would really give these calk-brained, rattle-jawed gossip-peddlars, who are about to lose their teeth, something to talk about."

He managed with an energy that came, Raederle suspected, from a dread of glimpsing among the river traffic that taut, brilliant sail of an Ymris war-ship, to secure by evening a barge, a crew and supplies. She, Lyra, Tristan and the guards returned after a hectic afternoon among curious traders, trappers and Osterland farmers, to find their horses and gear being transferred onto the barge. They boarded the flat, inelegant vessel, found room almost on top of one another to sleep. The barge, lifting to the shift of the tide at some black hour of the morning, left Kraal behind as they slept.

The trip upriver was long, tedious and grim. The waters had flooded villages and farms as they spilled down from the Ose. They were withdrawing slowly, leaving in their wake gnarled, sodden, uprooted trees, dead animals, fields of silt and mud. Bri had to stop frequently, cursing, to loosen snags of roots, branches and broken furniture that got in their way. Once, an oarsman, pushing them away from a dark, tangled mound, freed something that stared at the sun out of a dead-white, shapeless face a moment before the current whirled it away. Raederle, her throat closing, heard Tristan's gasp. The waters themselves in the constant flickering shadows of trees, seemed lifeless, grey as they flowed down from the High One's threshold. After a week of glimpsing, between the trees, men clearing pieces of barn and carcasses of farm animals out of their fields, and watching nameless things lift to eye level out of the deep water at the stir of an oar, even the guards began to look haggard. Lyra whispered once to Raederle, "Did it come like this down from Erlenstar Mountain? This frightens me."

At the fork, where the Winter River broke away from the Ose, the waters cleared finally with the brisk, blue-white current. Bri anchored at the fork, for the barge could go no farther, unloaded their gear and sent the barge back down the silent, shadowed river.

Tristan, watching it disappear into the trees, murmured, "I don't care if I have to walk home; I am not going on that river again." Then she turned, lifting her head to see the green face of Isig Mountain rising like a sentinel before the Pass. They seemed to be surrounded by mountains, the great mountain at whose roots the Osterland King lived, and the cold, distant peaks beyond the dead northern wastes. The morning sun was blazing above the head of Erlenstar Mountain, still glittering with unmelted snow. The light seemed to fashion the shadows, valleys, granite peaks that formed the Pass into the walls of some beautiful house lying open to the world.

Bri, his tongue full of names and tales he had not spoken for years, led them on horseback up the final stretch of river before the Pass. The bright, warm winds coming out of the backlands of the realm drove to the back of their memories the grey, dragging river behind them, and the secret, unexpected things dredged from its depths.

They found lodgings for a night in a tiny town that lay under the shadow of Isig. The next afternoon, they reached Kyrth, and saw at last the granite pillars honed by the Ose that were the threshold of Isig Pass. The sunlight seemed to leap goatlike from peak to peak; the air crackled white with the smell of melting ice. They had paused at a curve of road that led on one hand to Kyrth, on the other across a bridge to Isig. Raederle lifted her head. The ancient trees about them rose endlessly, face merging into face up the mountain, until they blurred together against the sky. Nearly hidden in them was a house with dark, rough walls and towers, windows that seemed faceted like jewels with color. Ribbons of smoke were coming up from within the walls; on the road a cart wheeled in and out of the trees toward it. The arch of its gates, massive and formidable as the gateway into the Pass, opened to the heart of the mountain.

"You'll need supplies," Bri Corbett said, and

Raederle brought her thoughts out of the trees with an effort.

"For what?" she asked a little wearily. His saddle creaked as he turned to gesture towards the Pass. Lyra nodded.

"He's right. We can hunt and fish along the way, but we need some food, more blankets, a horse for Tristan." Her voice sounded tired, too, oddly timbreless in the hush of the mountains. "There will be no place for us to stay until we reach Erlenstar Mountain."

"Does the High One know we're coming?" Tristan asked abruptly, and they all glanced involuntarily at the Pass.

"I suppose so," Raederle said after a moment. "He must. I hadn't thought about it."

Bri, looking a little nervous, cleared his throat. "You're going just like that through the Pass."

"We can't sail and we can't fly; have you got any better suggestions?"

"I do. I suggest you tell someone your intentions before you ride headlong into what was a death trap for the Prince of Hed. You might inform Danan Isig you're in his land and about to go through the Pass. If we don't come back out, at least someone in the realm will know where we vanished."

Raederle looked again up at the enormous house of the King, ageless and placid under the vibrant sky. "I don't intend to vanish," she murmured. "I can't believe we're here. That's the great tomb of the Earth-Master's children, the place where the stars were shaped and set into a destiny older than the realm itself . . ." She felt Tristan stir behind her; saw, in her shadow on the ground, the mute shake of her head.

"This couldn't have anything to do with Morgon!" she burst out, startling them. "He never knew anything about land like this. You could drop Hed like a button in it and never see it. How could—how could something have reached that far, across mountains and rivers and the sea, to Hed, to put those stars on his face?"

"No one knows that," Lyra said with unexpected gentleness. "That's why we're here. To ask the High One." She looked at Raederle, her brows raised questioningly. "Should we tell Danan?"

"He might argue. I'm in no mood to argue. That's a house with only one door, and none of us knows what Danan Isig is like. Why should we trouble him with things he can't do anything about anyway?" She heard Bri's sigh and added, "You could stay in Kyrth while we go through the Pass. Then, if we don't return, at least you'll know." His answer was brief and pithy; she raised her brows. "Well, if that's the way you feel about it . . ."

Lyra turned her horse toward Kyrth. "We'll send a message to Danan."

Bri tossed his objections into the air with his hands. "A message," he said morosely. "With this town crammed to the high beams with traders, the gossip will reach him before any message does."

Reaching the small city, they found his estimations of the traders' skills well-founded. The city curved to one side of the Ose, its harbor full of river-boats and barges heavily laden with furs, metals, weapons, fine plate, cups, jewels from Danan's house, straining against their moorings to follow the flood waters. Lyra dispatched three of the guards to find a horse for Tristan, and the others to buy what food and cooking pots they might need. She found in a smelly tanners' street, hides for them to sleep on, and in a cloth shop, fur-lined blankets. Contrary to Bri's expectations, they were rarely recognized, but in a city whose merchants, traders and craftsmen had been immobilized through a long, harsh winter into boredom, their faces caused much cheerful comment. Bri, growling ineffectually, was recognized himself, and crossed the street while Raederle paid for the blankets, to speak to a friend in a tavern doorway. They lingered a little in the clothshop examining the beautiful furs and strange, thick wools. Tristan hovered wistfully near a bolt of pale green wool until a grim, wild expression appeared suddenly on her face and she bought enough for three skirts. Then, laden to the chin with bundles, they stepped back into the street and looked for Bri Corbett.

"He must have gone in the tavern," Raederle said, and added a little irritably, for her feet hurt and she could have used a cup of wine, "He might have waited for us." She saw then, above the small tavern, the dark, endless rise of granite cliff and the Pass, itself, blazing with a glacial light as the last rays of the sun struck peak after icy peak. She took a breath of the lucent air, touched with a chill of fear at the awesome sight, and wondered for the first time since she had left An, if she had the courage to come face-to-face with the High One.

The light faded as they watched; shadows slipped after it, patching the Pass with purple and grey. Only one mountain, far in the distance, still burned white in some angle of light. The sun passed finally beyond the limits of the world, and the great flanks and peaks of the mountain turned to a smooth, barren whiteness, like the moon. Then Lyra moved slightly, and Raederle remembered she was there.

"Was that Erlenstar?" Lyra whispered.

"I don't know." She saw Bri Corbett come out of the tavern, then cross the street. His face looked oddly somber; he seemed as he reached them and stood looking at them, at a loss for words. His face was sweating a little in the cool air; he took his cap off, ran his fingers through his hair, and replaced it.

Then he said for some reason to Tristan, "We're

going to Isig Mountain, now, to talk to Danan Isig."

"Bri, what's wrong?" Raederle asked quickly. "Is there—is it something in the Pass?"

"You're not going through the Pass. You're going home."

"What?"

"I'm taking you home tomorrow; there's a keel-boat going down the Ose—"

"Bri," Lyra said levelly. "You are not taking any-one as far as the end of the street without an explanation."

"You'll get enough of one, I think, from Danan." He bent unexpectedly, put his hands on Tristan's shoulders, and the familiar, stubborn expression on her face wavered slightly. He lifted one hand, groped for his hat again, and knocked it into the street. He said softly, "Tristan . . ." and Raederle's hand slid suddenly over her mouth.

Tristan said warily, "What?"

"I don't . . . I don't know how to tell you."

The blood blanched out of her face. She stared back at Bri and whispered, "Just tell me. Is it Eliard?"

"No. Oh, no. It's Morgon. He's been seen in Isig, and, three days ago, in the King's court in Oster-land. He's alive."

Lyra's fingers locked in a rigid, painful grip above Raederle's elbow. Tristan's head bent, her hair brushing over her face. She stood so quietly they did not realize she was crying until her breath caught with a terrible sound in her throat, and Bri put his arms around her.

Raederle whispered, "Bri?" and his face turned to her.

"Danan Isig himself gave word to the traders. He can tell you. The trader I spoke to said—other things. You should hear them from Danan."

"All right," she said numbly. "All right." She

took Tristan's cloth from her as Bri led them toward the horses. But she turned to see the dark, startled expression in Lyra's eyes and, beyond her, the darkness moving down the Pass in the wake of the silvery Ose.

They found two of the guards before they left the city. Lyra asked them briefly to find lodgings in Kyrth; they accepted the situation without comment, but their faces were puzzled. The four followed the road across the bridge up the face of the mountain, which had settled into a shadowy, inward silence that the beat of their horse's hooves on the dead pine needles never penetrated. The road's end ran beneath the stone archway into Danan's courtyard. The many workshops, kilns and forges all seemed quiet, but as they rode through the darkened yard, one of the workshop doors opened suddenly. Torchlight flared out of it; a young boy, gazing at the metalwork in his hands, stepped under the nose of Bri's horse.

Bri reined sharply as the horse startled; the boy, glancing up in surprise, put an apologetic hand on the horse's neck and it quieted. He blinked at them, a broad-shouldered boy with black, blunt hair and placid eyes. "Everyone's eating," he said. "May I tell Danan who has come, and will you eat with us?"

"You wouldn't be Rawl Ilet's son, would you?" Bri asked a little gruffly. "With that hair?"

The boy nodded. "I'm Bere."

"I am Bri Corbett, ship-master of Mathom of An. I used to sail with your father, when I was a trader. This is Mathom's daughter, Raederle of An; the Morgol's land-heir, Lyra; and this is Tristan of Hed."

Bere's eyes moved slowly from face to face. He made a sudden, uncharacteristic movement, as though he had quelled an impulse to run shouting

101

for Danan. Instead he said, "He's just in the hall.
I'll get him—" He stopped speaking abruptly, a
jump of excitement in his voice, and went to Tristan's side. He held her stirrup carefully for her; she
gazed down at his bent head in amazement a moment before she dismounted. Then he yielded and
ran across the dark yard, flung the hall doors open
to a blare of light and noise, and they heard his
voice ringing above it: "Danan! Danan!" Bri, seeing the puzzled look on Tristan's face, explained
softly, "Your brother saved his life."

The King of Isig followed Bere out. He was a
big, broad man whose ash-colored hair glinted with
traces of gold. His face was brown and scarred like
tree bark, touched with an imperturbable calm that
seemed on the verge of being troubled as he looked
at them.

"You are most welcome to Isig," he said. "Bere,
take their horses. I'm amazed that the three of you
travelled so far together, and yet I've heard not a
word of your coming."

"We were on our way to Erlenstar Mountain,"
Raederle said. "We didn't give anyone word of our
leaving. We were buying supplies in Kyrth when
Bri—when Bri gave us a piece of news that we
could scarcely believe. So we came here to ask you
about it. About Morgon."

She felt the King's eyes study her face in the
shadows a moment, and she remembered then that
he could see in the dark. He said, "Come in," and
they followed him into the vast inner hall. A weave
of fire and darkness hung like shifting tapestries on
the walls of solid stone. The cheerful voices of
miners and craftsmen seemed fragmented, muted
in the sheer silence of stone. Water wound in flaming, curved sluices cut through the floor, trailed
lightly into darkness; torchlight spattered across
raw jewels thrusting out of the walls. Danan

stopped only to give a murmured instruction to a servant, then led them up a side staircase that spiralled through the core of a stone tower. He stopped at a doorway, drew back hangings of pure white fur.

"Sit down," he urged them, as they entered. They found places on the chairs and cushions covered with fur and skins. "You look worn and hungry; food will be brought up, and I'll tell you while you eat what I can."

Tristan, her face quiet again, bewildered with wonder, said suddenly to Danan, "You were the one who taught him how to turn into a tree."

He smiled. "Yes."

"That sounded so strange in Hed. Eliard couldn't understand how Morgon did it. He used to stop and stare up at the apple trees; he said he didn't know what Morgon did with—with his hair, and how could he breathe—Eliard." Her hands tightened on the arms of her chair; they saw the flash of joy in her eyes that was constantly tempered by a wariness. "Is he all right? Is Morgon all right?"

"He seemed so."

"But I don't understand," she said almost pleadingly. "He lost the land-rule. How can he be alive? And if he's alive, how can he be all right?"

Danan opened his mouth, closed it again as servants entered with great trays of food and wine, bowls of water. He waited while the fire was laid against the cool mountain evening, and they had washed and begun to eat a little. Then he said gently, as though he were telling a story to one of his grandchildren, "A week ago, walking across my empty yard at twilight, I found someone coming towards me, someone who seemed to shape himself, as he moved, out of the twilight, the ember smoke, the night shadows, someone I never again thought to see in this world. . . . When I first recognized Morgon, I felt for a moment as though he had just left my house and come back, he looked that familiar. Then, when I brought him into the light, I saw how he was worn to the bone, as if he had been burned from within by some thought, and how his hair was touched, here and there, with white. He talked to me far into the night, telling me many things, and yet it seemed that there was always some dark core of memory he would not open to me. He said that he knew he had lost the land-rule and asked for news of Hed, but I could tell him almost nothing. He asked me to give word to the traders that he was alive, so that you would know."

"Is he coming home?" Tristan asked abruptly. Danan nodded.

"Eventually, but . . . he told me he was using every shade of power he had learned just to stay alive—"

Lyra leaned forward. "What do you mean 'learned'? Ghisteslwchlohm taught him things?"

"Well, in a way. Inadvertently." Then his brows pulled together. "Now, how did you know that? Who it was that had trapped Morgon?"

"My mother guessed. Ghisteslwchlohm had also been one of the Masters at Caithnard when Morgon studied there."

"Yes. He told me that." They saw something harden in the peaceful eyes. "You see, apparently the Founder of Lungold was looking for something in Morgon's mind, some piece of knowledge, and in probing every memory, every thought, burning away at the deep, private places of it, he opened his own mind and Morgon saw his vast reserves of power. That's how he broke free of Ghisteslwchlohm at last, by drawing from the wizard's mind the knowledge of his strengths and weaknesses, using his own power against him. He said, near the end, at times he did not know which mind belonged to whom, especially after the wizard stripped out of him all instinct for the land-rule. But at the moment he attacked finally, he remembered his name, and knew that in the long, black, terrible year he had grown stronger than even the Founder of Lungold . . ."

"What about the High One?" Raederle said. Something had happened in the room, she felt; the solid stones circling the firelight, the mountains surrounding the tower and the house seemed oddly fragile; the light itself a whim of the darkness crouched at the rim of the world. Tristan's head was bent, her face hidden behind her hair; Raederle knew she was crying soundlessly. She felt something beginning to break in her own throat, and she clenched her hands against it. "What . . . Why didn't the High One help him?"

Danan drew a deep breath. "Morgon didn't tell me, but from things he did say, I think I know."

"And Deth? The High One's harpist?" Lyra whispered. "Did Ghisteslwchlohm kill him?"

"No," Danan said, and at the tone in his voice even Tristan lifted her head. "As far as I know he's alive. That was one thing Morgon said he wanted to do before he went back to Hed. Deth betrayed Morgon, led him straight into Ghisteslwchlohm's hands, and Morgon intends to kill him."

Tristan put her hands over her mouth. Lyra broke a silence brittle as glass, rising, stumbling into her chair as she turned. She walked straight across the room until a window intruded itself in her path, and she lifted both hands, laid them flat against it. Bri Corbett breathed something inaudible. Raederle felt the tears break loose in spite of the tight grip of her hands; she said, struggling at least to control her voices, "That doesn't sound like either one of them."

"No," Danan Isig said, and again she heard the hardness in his voice. "The stars on Morgon's face were of some thought born in this mountain, the stars on his sword and his harp cut here a thousand years before he was born. We're touching the edge of doom, and it may be that the most we can hope for is an understanding of it. I have chosen to place whatever hope I have in those stars and in that Star-Bearer from Hed. For that reason I have complied with his request that I no longer welcome the High One's harpist into my house or allow him to set foot across the boundaries of my land. I have given this warning to my own people and to the traders to spread."

Lyra turned. Her face was bloodless, tearless. "Where is he? Morgon?"

"He told me he was going to Yrye, to talk to Har. He is being tracked by shape-changers; he moves painstakingly from place to place, taking shape after shape out of fear. As soon as he left my doorstep at midnight he was gone—a brush of ash, a small night animal—I don't know what he became." He was silent a moment, then added wearily, "I told him to forget about Deth, that the wizards would kill him eventually, that he had greater powers in the world to contend with; but he told me that sometimes, as he lay sleepless in that place, his mind drained, exhausted from Ghisteslwchlohm's probing, clinging to despair like a hard rock because that was the only thing he knew belonged to him, he could hear Deth piecing together new songs on his harp . . . . Ghisteslwchlohm, the shape-changers, he can in some measure understand, but Deth he cannot. He has been hurt deeply, he is very bitter . . ."

"I thought you said he was all right," Tristan whispered. She lifted her head. "Which way is Yrye?"

"Oh, no," Bri Corbett said emphatically. "No. Besides, he's left Yrye, by now, surely. Not one step farther north are any of you going. We're sailing straight back down the Winter to the sea, and then home. All of you. Something in this smells like a hold full of rotten fish."

There was a short silence. Tristan's eyes were hidden, but Raederle saw the set, stubborn line of her jaw. Lyra's back was an inflexible, unspoken argument. Bri took his own sounding of the silence and looked satisfied.

Raederle said quickly before anyone could disillusion him, "Danan, my father left An over a month ago in the shape of a crow, to find out who killed the Star-Bearer. Have you seen or heard anything of him? I think he was heading for Erlenstar Mountain; he might have passed this way."

"A crow."

"Well, he—he is something of a shape-changer."

Danan's brows pulled together. "No. I'm sorry. Did he go directly there?"

"I don't know. It's always been difficult to know what he's going to do. But why? Surely Ghisteslwchlohm wouldn't be anywhere near the Pass, now." A memory came to her then, of the silent grey waters of the Winter coming down from the Pass, churning faceless, shapeless forms of death up from its shadows. Something caught at her voice; she whispered, "Danan, I don't understand. If Deth has been with Ghisteslwchlohm all this year, why didn't the High One warn us, himself, about him? If I told you that we intended to leave tomorrow, go through the Pass to Erlenstar Mountain to talk to the High One, what advice would you give us?"

She saw his hand lift in a little, quieting gesture. "Go home," he said gently. But he would not meet her eyes. "Let Bri Corbett take you home."

She sat late that night, thinking, after they had
finished talking, and Danan's daughter, Vert, had
taken them to small, quiet rooms in the tower to
sleep in. The thick stones were chilly; the mountain had not fully emerged into spring, and she had
lit a small fire laid in the hearth. She gazed into
the restless flames, her arms around her knees. The
fire flickered like thoughts in her eyes. Out of it
rose fragments of knowledge she had; she wove
them back and forth into one shapelessness after
another. Somewhere far beneath her, she knew,
hardened forever into memory, were the dead children of the Earth-Masters; the fire shivering over
her hands might have drawn their faces out of their
private blackness, but never warmed them. The
stars that had grown in that same darkness, that
had been brought to light and given their own pattern in Danan's house, would have burned like
questions in the flame, but of their own place in a
greater pattern they offered little answer. The
thought of them lit her mind like the blue-white
stone Astrin had given her; she saw again the
strange face always on the verge of turning towards
her, moving into identity. Another face shifted into
her mind: the private, austere face of a harpist who
had placed her uncertain fingers on her first flute,
who had, with his flawless harping and vigilant
mind, been the emissary of the High One for centuries. The face had been a mask; the friend who
had led Morgon out of Hed, down the last steps to
near-destruction, had been for centuries a stranger.

She shifted; the flames broke apart and rejoined.
Things did not match, nothing seemed logical.
Ylon leaped in her mind, at the sea's harping; the
sea he came out of had given her and Mathom
gifts of power; it had nearly given Morgon his
death. Something in her had wept with a memory
at the sight of the ruined city at King's Mouth

Plain; something in her had wrenched at her mind
for the dangerous knowledge in the core of the
small blue stone. Morgon had ridden towards the
High One's house, and the High One's harpist had
twisted his path into horror. A wizard had ripped
from his mind the right he had been born with;
the land-law, which no one but the High One could
alter, and the High One had done nothing. She
closed her eyes, feeling the prick of sweat at her
hairline. Deth had acted in the High One's name
for five centuries; he had been given nothing less,
in those centuries, than absolute trust. Following
some private pattern of his own, in an unprece-
dented, inconceivable act, he had conspired to destroy a land-ruler. The High One had occasionally,
in early days, dispensed doom for the simple intention. Why had he not acted against this man
who had betrayed him as well as the Star-Bearer?
Why had the High One not acted against Ghisteslwchlohm? Why . . . She opened her eyes, the
fire flaring painfully at her widened pupils, and
she blinked, seeing the room washed in flame. Why
had Ghisteslwchlohm, who had the whole of the
backlands of the realm to hide in, and who should
have felt the need to hide, kept Morgon so close
to Erlenstar Mountain? Why, when Deth had
harped to himself that long year while Morgon
clung to the despair that was his life, had the High
One never heard that harping? Or had he?

She stumbled to her feet, away from the hot
flames, away from an answer, impossible, appal-
ling, on the verge of language in her mind. The
hangings moved aside so quietly in the doorway
that their movement seemed almost an illusion of
the fire. She thought, barely seeing a dark-haired
woman in the half-light, that it was Lyra. Then,
staring into the dark, quiet eyes of the woman,
something settled into place deep within her, like a

stone falling to a ponderous silence on the ground floor of Isig Mountain.

She whispered, scarcely realizing she spoke, "I thought so."

6

SHE FELT HER MIND INVADED, PROBED SKILL-
fully. This time, when the image in the stone
reappeared, drawn out of memory, with the elusive, unfamiliar face, she did not struggle. She
waited as the woman was waiting, for the movement, the turn of the head towards her that would
name that face, put a name also to its irrevocable
doom. But he seemed frozen in her last glimpse of
him; the invisible rush towards him was caught,
stilled in motion. The image faded finally; the
woman drew out other memories, bright, random
scenes from Raederle's past. She saw herself as a
child again, talking to the pigs while Cyone talked
to the pig-woman; running through Madir's woods
effortlessly recognizing tree and the illusion of tree
while Duac and Rood shouted in frustration behind her; arguing with Mathon over the endless
riddles he had her learn while the summer sun lay
on the stones at her feet like an immutable golden
disc. The woman lingered long over her relation-
ship with the pig-woman, the small magic things the
pig-woman taught her; Mathom's marriage plans for
her seemed to intrigue the woman also, as well as

his imperturbable stubbornness against the opposition he faced from the lords of An, from Duac, from Cyone, from Raederle herself when she understood at last what he had done. A dark, weary tower in Aum rose unbidden in her mind, an isolated shadow in an oak wood; the woman loosed her at that point, and Raederle felt that for the first time, she was surprised.

"You went there. To Peven's tower."

Raederle nodded. The fire had coiled down into the embers; she was trembling as much from weariness as from the chill. The woman seemed to hover, mothlike, on the edge of the faint light. She glanced at the fire, and it sprang alive, lean and white, etching the quiet, delicate face again out of the darkness.

"I had to. I had to know what price my father had set to my name before I was ever born. So I went there. I couldn't go in, though. It was a long time ago; I was afraid . . ." She shook her head slightly, bringing her own thoughts back from the memory. She faced the woman again across the strange fire; the white flame twisted and burned in the depths of the still eyes. "Who are you? Something in me knows you."

"Ylon." The flame curved into something of a smile. "We are kinswomen, you and I."

"I know." Her voice sounded dry, hollow; her heart was beating its own hollow place within her. "You have had many kinsmen in the line of the Kings of An. But what are you?"

The woman sat beside the hearth; she lifted one hand to the flame in a gesture at once beautiful and childlike, then said, "I am a shape-changer. I killed Eriel Ymris and took her shape; I half-blinded Astrin Ymris; I came very close to killing the Star-Bearer, although it was not his death I was

112

interested in. Then. I am not interested in yours, if you are wondering."

"I was," Raederle whispered. "What—what is it you are interested in?"

"The answer to a riddle."

"What riddle?"

"You'll see it yourself, soon enough." She was silent, her eyes on the fire, her hands still in her lap, until Raederle's own eyes went to the flame, and she groped for the chair behind her. "It's a riddle old as the crevices of old tree roots, as the silence molding the groins of inner Isig, as the stone faces of the dead children. It is essential, as wind or fire. Time means nothing to me, only the long moment between the asking of that riddle and its answer. You nearly gave it to me, on that ship, but you broke the binding between you and the stone in spite of me. That surprised me."

"I didn't—I couldn't break it. I remember. Lyra hit me. You. That was you in my mind. And the riddle: You need to put a name to that face?"

"Yes."

"And then—and then what? What will happen?"

"You are something of a riddler. Why should I play your game for you?"

"It's not a game! You are playing with our lives!"

"Your lives mean nothing to me," the woman said dispassionately. "The Star-Bearer and I are looking for answers to the same questions: he kills when he needs to; our methods are no different. I need to find the Star-Bearer. He has grown very powerful and very elusive. I thought of using you or Tristan as bait to trap him, but I will let him make his own path awhile. I think I can see where it's leading him."

"He wants to kill Deth," Raederle said numbly.

"It won't be the first great harpist he has killed.

But he dare not turn his attention from Ghistesl-wchlohm too long, either. Morgon or the wizards must kill the Founder. The wizards themselves, from the way they are secretly moving towards Lungold, have a revenge of their own to satisfy. They will no doubt destroy one another, which will not matter; they've scarcely been alive for seven centuries." She caught the expression on Raederle's face, the words she swallowed, and smiled. "Nun? I watched her at Lungold, the powerful, the beautiful. She would hardly call herding pigs and making grass nets living."

"What would you call what you're doing?"

"Waiting." She was silent a moment, her imperturbed eyes on Raederle's face. "Are you curious about yourself? Of the extent of your own powers? They are considerable."

"No."

"I have been honest with you."

Raederle's hands loosened on the arms of her chair. Her head bowed; she felt again, at the woman's words, the odd sense of kinship, if not trust, an inescapable understanding. She said softly, the despair settling through her again, "Ylon's blood has been in my family for generations; no one, however troubled by it, ever realized that he was anything more than the son of a sea legend, just another inexplicable shape of the magic of An. Now I know what his father was. One of you. That gives me some kinship with you. But nothing else, nothing of your compassionlessness, your destructiveness—"

"Only our power." She shifted forward slightly. "Ylon's father and I tried to do the same thing: to disturb the land-rule of An and Ymris by giving their kings heirs of mixed blood and twisted instinct. It was for a purpose, and it failed. The land saw to its own. Only Ylon bore the torment of land-rule; his power dissipated in his descendants, grew unused, dormant. Except in you. One day, perhaps, you could put a name to that power, and that name would surprise you. But you will not live that long. You only know of Ylon's sadness. But have you ever wondered, if we are so terrible, what made him break out of his prison to return to us?"

"No," Raederle whispered.

"Not compassion, but passion . . ." Something in her voice opened then, like a flick of light in the deep of Isig opening a vein of unexpected richness to view, and she stopped. She reached down, touched the white fire with one hand, drew it softly into a glistening spider's web, a polished bone, a scattering of stars, a moon-white chambered shell, shape weaving into shape, falling from her hand, a handful of blazing flowers, a net knotted and glinting as with seawater, a harp with thin, glistening strings. Raederle, watching, felt a hunger stir in her, a longing to possess the knowledge of the fire, the fire itself. The woman's face had grown oblivious of her, intent on her work; it seemed touched with wonder itself at each fiery, beautiful shape. She let the fire fall at last like drops of water or tears back into the bed. "I take my power, as you take yours, from the heart of things, in a recognition of each thing. From the inward curve of a grass blade, from the pearl troubling as a secret deed in the oyster shell, from the scent of trees. Is that so unfamiliar to you?"

"No." Her voice seemed to come from a distance, somewhere beyond the small room, the shadowed stones. The woman continued softly,

"You can know it: the essence of fire. You have the power. To recognize it, to hold it, shape it, even to become fire, to melt into its great beauty, bound to no man's laws. You are skilled with illusion; you have played with a dream of the sun's fire. Now work with fire itself. See it. Understand it. Not with your eyes or your mind, but with the power in you to know and accept, without fear, without question, the thing as itself. Lift your hand. Hold it out. Touch the fire."

Raederle's hand moved slowly. For a moment the shifting, bone-white, lawless thing before her that she had known all her life yet never known, seemed, as it wove in and out of the darkness, a child's riddle. She reached out to it tentatively, curiously. Then she realized that, in reaching towards it, she was turning away from her own name—the familiar heritage in An that had defined her from her birth —towards a heritage that held no peace, a name that no one knew. Her hand, curved to the flame, closed abruptly. She felt the heat, the fire's barrier, then, and drew back from it quickly. Her voice broke from her.

"No."

"You can, when you choose. When you lose your fear of the source of your power."

"And then what?" She brought her eyes away from her hand with an effort. "Why are you telling me that? Why do you care?"

Something moved minutely in the planes of the face, as though far away, in the darkness, the door of a thought had closed. "For no reason. I was curious. About you, about your father's vow binding you to the Star-Bearer. Was that foreknowledge?"

"I don't know."

"The Star-Bearer, I expected, but not you. Will you tell him, or will you let him guess, if you ever see him again, that you are kin to those trying to destroy him? If you ever bear him children, will you tell him whose blood they carry?"

Raederle swallowed. Her throat felt dry, her skin stretched taut and dry as parchment across her face. She had to swallow again before her voice would come. "He is a riddle-master. He won't need to be told." She found herself on her feet then, with the hollow in her growing deep, unbearable. She turned blindly away from the woman. "So he'll win me with one riddle and lose me with another," she added, hardly realizing what she was saying. "Is that any of your business?"

"Why else am I here? You are afraid to touch Ylon's power; then remember his longing."

The hopeless sorrow struck like a tide, welled through Raederle until she saw nothing, heard nothing, felt nothing but the grief and longing that had filled her at the sight of King's Mouth Plain. But she could not escape from it; her own sorrow was woven to it. She smelled then the bitter smell of the sea, dried kelp, iron rusted with the incessant spray that Ylon must have smelled; heard the hollow boom of the tide against the foundation stones of his tower, the suck of it bearing back from the green, pointed teeth of rocks below him. She heard the lament of sea birds wheeling aimlessly to the wind. Then she heard out of a world beyond eyesight, a world beyond hope, a harping tuned to her grief, playing back, in sympathy, her own lament. It was a fragile harping, almost lost in the brush of rain over the sea, on the flow and ebb of the tide. She found herself straining to hear it, moving towards it, straining, until her hands touched cold glass, as Ylon's hands would have touched the iron bars over his window. She blinked away the harping, the sea; it receded slowly. The woman's voices receded with it.

"We are all tuned to that harping. Morgon killed the harpist, Ylon's father. So where, in a world of such unexpected shape, will you put your certainty?"

The silence at her leaving was like the full,

charged silence before a storm. Raederle, still standing at the window, took one step towards the doorway. But Lyra could give her no help, perhaps not even understanding. She heard a sound break out of her, shiver across the silence, and she held it back with her hands. A face slipped into her thoughts: a stranger's face now, worn, bitter, troubled, itself. Morgon could not help her, either, but he had weathered truth, and he could face, with her, one more thing. Her hands had begun to move before she realized it, emptying the clothes from her pack, scattering the fruit, nuts and sweetmeats on the wine table into it, pushing on top of them a soft skin lying across one of the chairs, buckling the pack again. She threw her cloak over her shoulders and went silently out of the room, leaving behind her like a message the white, twisting flame.

She could not find the stables in the dark, so she walked out of the King's yard, down the mountain road in the thin moonlight to the Ose. She remembered from Bri's maps, how the Ose ran southward a little, curving around the foothills behind Isig; she could follow it until it began to turn east. Morgon would be heading south, down from Osterland, carrying his tale to Herun, she guessed; or was he, like the wizards, on his way to Lungold? It did not matter; he would have to go south, and with his wizard's mind alert to danger, perhaps he would sense her travelling alone and on foot in the backlands and investigate.

She found an old cart trail, rutted and overgrown, running along the side of the river, and she followed it. At first, fleeing the King's house, her grieving had seemed to make her invisible, impervious to weariness, cold, fear. But the swift, insistent voice of the Ose brought her out of her thoughts, shivering into the dark. The moon patched the road with shadows, the voice of the river hid other voices, sounds she was not certain she heard, rustling that may or may not have come from behind her. The ancient pines with their calm, wrinkled faces, Danan's face, gave her comfort. She heard the crash and snarl of animals once, near her, and stopped short, then realized that she did not really care what might happen to her, and probably, neither did they. The river dragged the sound of their quarrel away. She walked on until the cart road ended abruptly in a clump of brambles, and the moon began to set. She unpacked the skin, lay down and covered herself. She slept, exhausted and heard in her dreams a harping above the constant movement of the Ose.

She woke at sunrise; her eyes burned at the touch of the sun. She splashed water from the river on her face and drank it, then ate a little food from her pack. Her bones ached; her muscles protested at every movement until she began to walk again and forgot about them. Making her own path down the river did not seem difficult; she skirted bramble patches, climbed over rocks when the banks rose steeply above it, gathered her torn skirts to wade when the bank was impassible, washed her bruised, scratched hands in the river and felt the sun beat down on her face. She ignored the time passing, intent on nothing but her own movement until it came to her, slowly and forcibly, that she was being followed.

She stopped then. All the weariness and ache of her body caught up with her, draining through her until she swayed, balanced on a rock in the river. She bent, drank water, and looked behind her again. Nothing moved through the lazy hot noon hour, and yet she sensed movement, her name in someone's mind. She drank again, wiped her mouth on her sleeve, and began to work out of it a piece of silver thread.

She left several of them in her trail, intricately

wound and tangled. She drew long grass blades together and knotted them; they looked fragile to the eye, but to a man or a horse tripping over them, they would seem strong as taut rope. She poised wayward stems of brambles over her path, seeing, in her mind's eye, the formidable prickly clumps they would seem to anyone else. In one place she dug a fist-sized hole, lined it with leaves, and then filled it with water she carried in her hands. It stared back at the blue sky like an eye, a round, unobtrusive pool that could stretch like a dream into a wide, impassible lake.

The nagging following began to be less urgent; she guessed that it had met with some of her traps. She slowed a little herself, then. It was late afternoon; the sun hovered above the tips of the pine. A little wind shivered through them, the cool evening wind, rousing. It carried a loneliness in its wake, the loneliness of the backlands. She glimpsed then the long succession of days and nights ahead of her, the lonely trek through the unsettled lands, nearly impossible for one weaponless, on foot. But behind her lay Isig Pass with its dark secret; in An there was no one, not even her father, to give her a measure of understanding. She could only hope that her blind need would stumble onto its own source of comfort. She shivered a little, not at the wind, but at the empty rustle of its passing, and went on. The sun set, drawing fingers of light through the trees; the twilight lay in an unearthly silence over the world. Still she moved, without thinking, without stopping to eat, without realizing that she walked on the thin line of exhaustion. The moon rose; her constant tripping over things she could not see in the dark began to slow her. She fell once, seemingly for no reason, and was surprised when she found it difficult to rise. She fell again, a few paces later, with the same surprise.

She felt blood trickle down her knee and put her hand in a patch of nettles as she rose. She stood nursing her hand under one arm, wondering why her body was shaking, for the night was not very cold. Then she saw, like a dream of hope, the warm, slender dance of flame within the trees. She went towards it with one name in her mind. Reaching it finally, she found in the circle of its light the High One's harpist.

For a moment, standing at the edge of the light, she saw only that it was not Morgon. He was sitting back against a rock beside the fire, his face bent; she saw only his silver-white hair. Then he turned his head and looked at her.

She heard his breath catch. "Raederle?"

She took a step backward, and he moved abruptly, as if to rise and stop her before she vanished again into the darkness. Then he checked himself, leaned back deliberately against the rock. There was an expression on his face she had never seen before, that kept her lingering at the light. He gestured to the fire, the hare spitted over it.

"You look tired; sit down awhile." He turned the spit; a breath of hot meat came to her. His hair was ragged; his face looked worn, lined, oddly open. His voice, musical and edged with irony, had not changed.

She whispered, "Morgon said that you—that you harped while he lay half-dead in Ghisteslwchlohm's power."

She saw the muscles in his face tighten. He reached out, edged a broken branch into the fire. "It's true. I will reap my reward for that harping. But meanwhile, will you have some supper? I am doomed; you are hungry. One has very little to do with the other, so there is no reason for you not to eat with me."

She took another step, this time towards him.

Though he watched her, his expression did not change, and she took another. He took a cup from his pack, filled it with wine from a skin. She came close finally, held out her hands to the blaze. They hurt her; she turned and saw the cuts on them from brambles, the white blisters from the nettles. His voice came again. "I have water . . ." It faded. She glanced down at him, watched him pour water from another skin into a bowl. His fingers shook slightly as he corked the skin; he did not speak again. She sat finally, washed the dirt and dried blood from her hands. He passed her wine, bread and meat in the same silence, sipped wine slowly while she ate.

Then he said, his voice sliding so evenly into the silence that it did not startle her, "Morgon, I expected to find in the night at my fire's edge, or any one of five wizards, but hardly the second most beautiful woman of the Three Portions of An."

She glanced down at herself absently. "I don't think I'm that any more." A pang of sorrow caught at her throat as she swallowed; she put the food down and whispered, "Even I have changed shape. Even you."

"I have always been myself."

She looked at the fine, elusive face, with its unfamiliar shadow of mockery. She asked then, for both the question and the answer seemed impersonal, remote, "And the High One? Whom have you harped to for so many centuries?"

He leaned forward almost abruptly to stir the lagging fire. "You know to ask the question; you know the answer. The past is the past. I have no future."

Her throat burned. "Why? Why did you betray the Star-Bearer?"

"Is it a riddle-game? I'll give answer for answer."

"No. No games."

They were silent again. She sipped her wine, felt, coming alive all through her, little aches and throbbings from cuts, pulled muscles, bruises. He filled her cup again when she finished. She broke the silence, easy in his presence for some reason, as though they sat together in the same black hollow of sorrow. "He already killed one harpist."

"What?"

"Morgon." She moved a little, shifting away from the longing the name gave her. "Ylon's father. Morgon killed Ylon's father."

"Ylon," he said tonelessly, and she lifted her head, met his eyes. Then he laughed, his hands linked hard around his cup. "So. That sent you into the night. And you think, in the midst of this chaos, that it matters?"

"It matters! I have inherited a shape-changer's power—I can feel it! If I reached out and touched the fire, I could hold it in the palm of my hand. Look . . ." Something: the wine, his indifference, her hopelessness, made her reckless. She stretched out her hand, held it curved in a motionless caress to the heat and curve of a flame. The reflection of it flickered in Deth's eyes; its light lay cradled in the lines and hollows of the stone he leaned against, traced the roots of ancient trees into untangling. She let the reflection ease through her thoughts, followed every shift of color and movement, every fade and mysterious renewal out of nothingness. It was of an alien fabric that ate darkness and never died. Its language was older than men. It was a shape-changer; it groped for the shape of her mind as she watched it, filled her eyes so that she saw a single leaf fall in a liquid, burning tear through the darkness to the ground. And deep within her, rousing out of a dormant, lawless heritage came the fiery, answering leap of understanding. The lucent, wordless knowledge of fire filled her; the soft rustlings became a language, the incessant weave a purpose, its color the color of the world, of her mind. She touched a flame then, let it lay in her hand like a flower. "Look," she said breathlessly, and closed her hand over it, extinguishing it, before the wonder in her broke the binding between them, separating them, and it hurt her. The night fell around her again, as the tiny flame died. She saw Deth's face, motionless, unreadable, his lips parted.

"Another riddle," he whispered.

She rubbed her palm against her knee, for in spite of her care it hurt a little. A breath of reason, like the cool air off the northern peaks brushed her mind; she shivered, and said slowly, remembering, "She wanted me to hold the fire, her fire . . ."

"Who?"

"The woman. The dark woman who had been Eriel Ymris for five years. She came to me to tell me we were kin, which I had already guessed."

"Mathom trained you well," he commented, "to be a riddle-master's wife."

"You were a Master. You told him that once. Am I so good with riddles? What do they lead to but betrayal and sorrow? Look at you. You not only betrayed Morgon, but my father and everyone in this realm who trusted you. And look at me. What lord of An would bother to draw enough breath to ask for me, if he knew who claimed kinship with me?"

"You are running from yourself, and I am running from death. So much for the tenets of riddle-mastery. Only a man with a brain and heart implacable as the jewels in Isig could bear adhering to them. I made my decision five centuries ago about the values of riddles, when Ghisteslwchlohm asked me to Erlenstar Mountain. I thought nothing in the realm could break his power. But I was wrong. He broke himself against the rigid tenets of the Star-Bearer's life and fled, leaving me alone, unprotected, harpless—"

"Where is your harp?" she asked, surprised.

"I don't know. Still in Erlenstar Mountain, I assume. I don't dare harp now. That was the only other thing Morgon heard, besides Ghisteslwchlohm's voice, for a year."

She flinched, wanting to run from him then, but her body would not move. She cried out at him, "Your harping was a gift to Kings!" He did not answer; his cup rose, flashed again in the firelight. When he spoke finally, his voice seemed shaded, like the fire's voice.

"I've played and lost to a Master; he'll take his vengeance. But I regret the loss of my harp."

"As Morgon must regret the loss of his land-rule?" Her own voice shook. "I'm curious about that. How could Ghisteslwchlohm rip that from him—the instinct for the land-law that is known only to Morgon and the High One? What piece of knowledge did the Founder expect to find beneath the knowledge of when the barley would begin to sprout or what trees in his orchard had a disease eating secretly at their hearts?"

"It's done. Can you let—"

"How can I? Did you think you were betraying only Morgon? You taught me 'The Love of Hover and Bird' on the flute when I was nine. You stood behind me and held my fingers down on the right notes while I played. But that hardly matters, compared to what the land-rulers of the realm will feel when they realize what honor they have given to the harpist of the Founder of Lungold. You hurt Lyra badly enough, but what will the Morgol, herself, think when Morgon's tale reaches her? You—" She stopped. He had not moved; he was sitting as she had first seen him, with his head bent, one hand on his bent knee, the cup cradled in it. Something

125

had happened to her, in her anger. She lifted her head, smelled the fine, chill, pine-scented air off Isig, felt the night that lay over her like its shadow. She sat at a tiny fire, lost in that vast blackness, her dress torn, her hair tangled and dirty, her face scratched, probably so haggard no Lord of An would recognize her. She had just put her hand in the fire and held it; something of its clarity seemed to burn in her mind. She whispered, "Say my name."

"Raederle."

Her own head bent. She sat quietly awhile, feeling the name in her like a heartbeat. She drew breath at last, loosed it. "Yes. That woman nearly made me forget. I ran from Isig in the middle of the night to look for Morgon somewhere in the backlands. It seems unlikely, doesn't it, that I'll find him that way."

"A little."

"And no one in Danan's house knows if I am alive or dead. That seems inconsiderate. I forgot that, having Ylon's power, I still have my own name. That's a very great power, that alone. The power to see . . ."

"Yes." He lifted his head finally, lifted the cup to drink again, but instead put it down with a curious care on the ground. He sat back, his face thrown clear in the light; the mockery in it had gone. She drew her knees together, huddling against herself, and he said, "You're cold. Take my cloak."

"No."

His mouth crooked slightly, but he said only, "What is Lyra doing in Isig Mountain?"

"We came to ask the High One questions— Lyra, Tristan of Hed, and I—but Danan told us that Morgon was alive, and he advised against going through the Pass. It took me hours to think why. And it has taken this long—a day and two nights

—to think of another question. But there's no one to ask, except Morgon, and you."

"You would trust me with a question?"

She nodded a little wearily. "I don't understand you any more; your face changes shape every time I look at you, now a stranger, now the face of a memory . . . But whoever you are, you still know as much, if not more, as anyone else about what is happening in the realm. If Ghisteslwchlohm took the High One's place at Erlenstar Mountain, then where is the High One? Someone still holds order in the realm."

"True." He was silent, an odd tautness to his mouth. "I asked Ghisteslwchlohm that five centuries ago. He couldn't answer me. So I lost interest. Now, with my own death inevitable, I am still not very interested, any more than the High One, where he is, seems remotely interested in any problems in the realm beyond land-law."

"Perhaps he never existed. Perhaps he's a legend spun out of the mystery of the ruined cities, passed through the ages until Ghisteslwchlohm took the shape of it . . ."

"A legend like Ylon? Legends have a grim way of twisting into truth."

"Then why did he never stop you from harping in his name? He must have known."

"I don't know. No doubt he has reasons. Whether he or Morgon dooms me, it makes little difference; the result will be the same."

"There's nowhere you can go?" she asked, surprising both herself and him. He shook his head.

"Morgon will close the realm to me. Even Herun. I will not go there, in any event. I was already driven out of Osterland, three nights ago, crossing the Ose. The wolfking spoke to his wolves . . . A pack found me camping on his land, a remote corner of it. They did not touch me, but they let me know I was not welcome. When word reaches Ymris, it will be the same. And An . . . The Star-Bearer will drive me where he wants me. I saw the hollow he made of the High One's house when he finally broke free—it seemed as if Erlenstar Mountain itself was too small to hold him. He paused, in passing, to wrench the strings out of my harp. His judgment of me I don't contest, but . . . that was one thing in my life I did well."

"No," she whispered. "You did many things well. Dangerously well. There wasn't a man, woman or child in the realm who didn't trust you: you did that well. So well that I am still sitting beside you, talking to you, even though you hurt someone I love past bearing. I don't know why."

"Don't you? It's simply that, alone in the backlands under a sky black as the pit of a dead king's eye, we have nothing left but our honesty. And our names. There is great richness in yours," he added almost lightly, "but not even hope in mine."

She fell asleep soon afterwards beside his fire, while he sat quietly drinking wine and feeding the fire. When she woke in the morning, he was gone. She heard rustlings in the brush, voices; she shifted painfully, freeing an arm to push back the covering over her. Then she checked. She sat up abruptly, staring down at her hand, in which the fire had burned like an extension of herself the night before. On her palm, scored white, were the twelve sides and delicate inner lines of the stone Astrin had given her on King's Mouth Plain.

7

L YRA, TRISTAN AND THE GUARDS RODE OUT OF
the trees, then, into the tiny clearing where
Raederle sat. Lyra reined sharply at the sight
of her, dismounted without a word. She looked dishevelled herself, worn and tired. She went to
Raederle, knelt beside her. She opened her mouth
to say something, but words failed her. She opened
her hand instead, dropped between them three
tangled, dirty pieces of thread.

Raederle stared down at them, touched them.
"That was you behind me," she whispered. She
straightened, pushing hair out of her eyes. The
guards were dismounting. Tristan, still on her horse,
was staring at Raederle, wide-eyed and frightened.
She slid to the ground abruptly, came to Raederle's
side.

"Are you all right?" Her voice was sharp with
worry. "Are you all right?" She brushed pieces of
pine needle and bark out of Raederle's hair gently.
"Did anyone hurt you?"

"Who were you running from?" Lyra asked.
"Was it a shape-changer?"

"Yes."

"What happened? I was just across the hall; I couldn't sleep. I didn't even hear you leave. I didn't hear—" She stopped abruptly, as at a memory. Raederle pushed wearily at the cloak that had been covering her; it was hot, heavy in the bright morning. She drew her knees up, dropping her face against them, feeling a complaint from every bone at the simple movements. The others were silent; she could feel their waiting, so she said haltingly after a moment,

"It was—one of the shape-changers came to my room, spoke to me. After she left, I wanted—I wanted to find Morgon very badly, to talk to him. I was not thinking very clearly. I left Danan's house, walked in the night until the moon set. Then I slept awhile and walked again, until—until I came here. I'm sorry about the traps."

"What did she say? What could she have said to make you run like that?"

Raederle lifted her head. "Lyra, I can't talk about it now," she whispered. "I want to tell you, but not now."

"All right." She swallowed. "It's all right. Can you get up?"

"Yes." Lyra helped her stand; Tristan reached for the cloak, bundled it in her arms, gazing anxiously over it.

Raederle glanced around. There seemed to be no trace of Deth; he had passed in and out of the night like a dream, but one of the guards, Goh, casting about with a methodical eye, said, "There was a horseman here." She gazed southward as if she were watching his passage. "He went that way. The horse might have been bred in An, from the size of the hoof. It's no plow horse, or Ymris war horse."

"Was it your father?" Lyra asked a little incredulously. Raederle shook her head. Then she seemed

130

to see for the first time the heavy, rich, blue-black cloak in Tristan's arms. Her teeth clenched; she took the cloak from Tristan, flung it into the ashes of the fire bed, seeing across from it as she did so, the harpist's face changing to every shift of firelight. Her hands locked on her arms; she said, her voice steady again, "It was Deth."

"Deth," Lyra breathed, and Raederle saw the touch of longing in her face. "He was here? Did you speak to him?"

"Yes. He fed me. I don't understand him. He told me that everything Morgon said about him is true. Everything. I don't understand him. He left his cloak for me while I was sleeping."

Lyra turned abruptly, bent to check the trail Goh had found. She stood again, looking southward. "How long ago did he leave?"

"Lyra," Imer said quietly, and Lyra turned to face her. "If you intend to track that harpist through the backlands of the realm, you'll go alone. It's time for us all to return to Herun. If we leave quickly enough, we can reach it before Morgon does, and you can ask him your questions. The tale itself will reach Herun before any of us do, I think, and the Morgol will need you."

"For what? To guard the borders of Herun against Deth?"

"It might be," Goh said soothingly, "that he has some explanation to give only to the Morgol."

"No," Raederle said. "He said he would not go to Herun."

They were silent. The wind roused, sweet-smelling, empty, stalking southward like a hunter. Lyra stared down at the cloak in the ashes. She said blankly, "I can believe he betrayed the Star-Bearer if I must, but how can I believe he would betray the Morgol? He loved her."

"Let's go," Kia urged softly. "Let's go back to

Herun. None of us knows any more what to do. This place is wild and dangerous; we don't belong here."

"I'm going to Herun," Tristan said abruptly, startling them with her decisiveness. "Wherever that is. If that's where Morgon is going."

"If we sail," Raederle said, "we might get there before he does. Is Bri— Where is Bri Corbett? He let you come after me alone?"

"We didn't exactly stop to ask his permission," Lyra said. The guards were beginning to mount again. "I brought your horse. The last time I saw Bri Corbett, he was searching the mines with Danan and the miners."

Raederle took her reins, mounted stiffly. "For me? Why did they think I would have gone into the mines?"

"Because Morgon did," Tristan said, "when he was there." She pulled herself easily onto the small, shaggy pony the guards had brought for her. Her face was still pinched with worry; she viewed even the genial profile of Isig with a disapproving eye. "That's what Danan said. I got up near morning to talk to you, because I had had a bad dream. And you were gone. There was only that fire, white as a turnip. It frightened me, so I woke Lyra. And she woke the King. Danan told us to stay in the house while he searched the mines. He was also afraid you had been kidnapped. But Lyra said you weren't."

"How did you know?" Raederle asked, surprised.

The guards had formed a loose, watchful circle around them as they rode back through the trees. Lyra said simply, "Why would you have taken your pack and all the food in the room if you had been kidnapped? It didn't make sense. So while Danan searched his house, I went into town and found the guards. I left a message for Danan, telling him where we were going. Finding your trail wasn't difficult; the ground is still soft, and you left pieces of cloth from your skirt on brambles beside the river. But then your horse stepped on one of the threads you dropped and pulled out of Goh's hold; we spent an hour chasing it. And after we caught it finally, Kia rode over another thread and went off into the brush before anyone saw her. So we spent more time tracking her. After that, I watched for your threads. But it took me awhile to realize why our horses kept stumbling over things that weren't there, and why there were mountains of brambles along the river that your footprints seemed to disappear into. And then we came to that lake . . ." She paused, giving the memory a moment of fulminous silence. The blood was easing back into Raederle's face as she listened.

"I'm sorry it was you. Was—Did it work?"

"It worked. We spent half an afternoon trying to round one shore of it. It was impossible. It simply didn't look that big. It just stretched. Finally Goh noticed that there were no signs that you had walked around it, and I realized what it might be. I was so hot and tired I got off my horse and walked straight into it; I didn't care if I got wet or not. And it vanished. I looked behind me, and saw all the dry ground we had been skirting, making a path around nothing."

"She stood in the middle of the water and cursed," Imer said, with a rare grin. "It looked funny. Then, when we reached the river again, to pick up your trail, and saw that tiny pool, no bigger than a fist, we all cursed. I didn't know anyone but a wizard could do that with water."

Raerderle's hand closed suddenly over its secret. "I've never done it before." The words sounded unconvincing to her ears. She felt oddly ashamed, as though, like Deth, she held a stranger's face to the world. The calm, ancient face of Isig rose over them, friendly in the morning light, its raw peaks gentled. She said with sudden surprise, "I didn't get very far, did I?"

"You came far enough," Lyra said.

They reached Isig again at noon the next day. Bri Corbett, grim and voluble with relief, took one look at Raederle, stayed long enough to hear Lyra's tale, then departed to find a boat at Kyrth. Raederle said very little, either to Danan or Bri; she was grateful that the mountain-king refrained from questioning her. He only said gently, with a perception that startled her, "Isig is my home; the home of my mind, and still, after so many years, it is capable of surprising me. Whatever you are gripping to yourself in secret, remember this: Isig holds great beauty and great sorrow, and I could not desire anything less for it, than that it yields always, unsparingly, the truth of itself."

Bri returned that evening, having wheedled places for them all, their horses and gear, on two keelboats packed and readied to leave for Kraal at dawn. The thought of another journey down the Winter made them all uneasy, but it was, when they finally got underway, not so terrible as before. The floodwaters had abated; the fresh, blue waters of the upper Ose pushed down it, clearing the silt and untangling the snags. The boats ran quickly on the crest of the high water; they could see, as the banks flowed past them, the Osterland farmers pounding the walls of their barns and pens back together again. The piquant air skimmed above the water, rippling it like the touch of birds' wings; the warm sun glinted off the metal hinges of the cargo chests, burned in flecks of spray on the ropes.

Raederle, scarcely seeing at all as she stood day after day at the rail, was unaware of her own disturbing silence. The evening before they were due to reach Kraal, she stood in the shadowy twilight under the lacework of many trees, and realized, only after the leaves had blurred into darkness, that Lyra was standing beside her. She started slightly.

Lyra, the weak light from the chart house rippling over her face, said softly, "If Morgon has already passed through Crown City when we get there, what will you do?"

"I don't know. Follow him."

"Will you go home?"

"No." There was a finality in her voice that surprised her. Lyra frowned down at the dark water, her proud, clean-lined face like a lovely profile on a coin. Raederle, looking at her, realized with helpless longing, the assuredness in it, the absolute certainty of place.

"How can you say that?" Lyra asked. "How can you not go home? That's where you belong, the one place."

"For you, maybe. You could never belong anywhere but in Herun."

"But you are of An! You are almost a legend of An, even in Herun. Where else could you go? You are of the magic of An, of the line of its kings; where . . . What did that woman say to you that is terrible enough to keep you away from your own home?"

Raederle was silent, her hands tightening on the rail. Lyra waited; when Raederle did not answer, she went on, "You have scarcely spoken to anyone since we found you in the forest. You have been holding something in your left hand since then. Something—that hurts you. I probably wouldn't understand it. I'm not good with incomprehensible things, like magic and riddling. But if there is something I can fight for you, I will fight it. If there is something I can do for you, I will do it. I swear that, on my honor—" Raederle's face turned abruptly toward her at the word, and she stopped.

Raederle whispered, "I've never thought about honor in my life. Perhaps it's because no one has ever questioned it in me, or in any of my family. But I wonder if that's what's bothering me. I would have little of it left to me in An."

"Why?" Lyra breathed incredulously. Raederle's hand slid away from the rail, turned upward, open to the light.

Lyra stared down at the small, angular pattern on her palm. "What is that?"

"It's the mark of that stone. The one I blinded the warships with. It came out when I held the fire—"

"You—she forced you to put your hand in the fire?"

"No. No one forced me. I simply reached out and gathered it in my hand. I knew I could do it, so I did it."

"You have that power?" Her voice was small with wonder. "It's like a wizard's power. But why are you so troubled? Is it something that the mark on your hand means?"

"No. I hardly know what that means. But I do know where the power has come from, and it's not from any witch of An or any Lungold wizard. It's from Ylon, who was once King of An, a son of a queen of An and a shapechanger. His blood runs in the family of An. I have his power. His father was the harpist who tried to kill Morgon in your house."

Lyra gazed at her, wordless. The chart house light flicked out suddenly, leaving their faces in darkness; someone lit the lamps at the bow. Raederle, her face turning back to the water, heard Lyra start to say something and then stop. A few minutes later, still leaning against the rail at Raederle's side, she started again and stopped.

Raederle waited for her to leave, but she did not move. Half an hour later, when they were both beginning to shiver in the nightbreeze, Lyra drew another breath and found words finally.

"I don't care," she said softly, fiercely. "You are who you are, and I know you. What I said still stands; I have sworn it, the same promise I would have given to Morgon if he hadn't been so stubborn. It's your own honor, not the lack of it, that is keeping you out of An. And if I don't care, why should Morgon? Remember who the source of half his power is. Now let's go below before we freeze."

They reached Kraal almost before the morning mists had lifted above the sea. The boats docked; their passengers disembarked with relief, stood watching the cargo being unloaded while Bri went to find Mathom's ship and sailors to load their gear again. Kia murmured wearily to no one, "If I never set foot on a ship again in my life, I will be happy. If I never see a body of water larger than the Morgol's fish pools . . ."

Bri came back with the sailors and led them to the long, regal ship swaying in its berth. After the barge and keelboats, it looked expansive and comfortable; they boarded gratefully. Bri, with one eye to the tide, barked orders contentedly from the bow, as the sailors secured what supplies they needed, stabled the horses, brought the gear from the keelboats and loaded it all again. Finally the long anchor chain came rattling out of the sea; the ship was loosed from its moorings, and the stately blue and purple sails of An billowed proudly above the river traffic.

Ten days later they docked at Hlurle. The Morgol's guards were there to meet them.

Lyra, coming down the ramp with the five guards behind her, stopped at the sight of the quiet, armed gathering on the dock. One of the guards, a tall, grey-eyed girl, said softly, "Lyra—"

Lyra shook her head. She lifted her spear, held it out in her open hands, quiescent and unthreatening, like an offering. Raederle, following, heard her say simply, "Will you carry my spear through Herun for me, Trika, and give it for me to the Morgol? I will resign when I get to Crown City."

"I can't."

Lyra looked at her silently, at the still faces of the fourteen guards behind Trika. She shifted slightly. "Why? Did the Morgol give you other orders? What does she want of me?"

Trika's hand rose, touched the spear briefly and fell. Behind Lyra, the five guards were lined, motionless, across the ramp, listening. "Lyra." She paused, choosing words carefully. "You have twenty witnesses to the fact that you were willing, for the sake of the honor of the Morgol's guards, to ride unarmed into Herun. However, I think you had better keep your spear awhile. The Morgol is not in Herun."

"Where is she? Surely she isn't still at Caithnard?"

"No. She came back from Caithnard over a month ago, took six of us with her back to Crown City, and told the rest of us to wait for you here. Yesterday, Feya came back with the news that she had—that she was no longer in Herun."

"Well, if she isn't in Herun, where did she go?"

"No one knows. She just left."

Lyra brought her spear down to rest with a little thump at her side. She lifted her head, picked out a lithe, red-haired guard with her eyes. "Feya, what do you mean she left?"

"She left, Lyra. One night she was there having

supper with us, and the next morning she was gone."

"She must have told someone where she was going. She never does things like that. Did she take servants, baggage, any guards at all?"

"She took her horse."

"Her horse? That's all?"

"We spent the day questioning everyone in the house. That's all she took. Not even a packhorse."

"Why didn't anyone see her leave? What were you all guarding, anyway?"

"Well, Lyra," someone said reasonably, "she knows the changes of our watch as well as any of us, and no one would ever question her movements in her own house."

Lyra was silent. She moved off the ramp, out of the way of the curious sailors beginning to unload their gear. Raederle, watching her, thought of the calm, beautiful face of the Morgol as she rode up the hill to the College, the gold eyes turning watchful as the Masters gathered around her. A question slid into her mind; Lyra, her brows crooking together, asked it abruptly, "Has Morgon of Hed spoken to her?"

Feya nodded. "He came so quietly no one saw him but the Morgol; he left just as quietly, except —except that—nothing was very peaceful in Herun after his leaving."

"She gave orders?" Her voice was level. Beside Raederle, Tristan sat down heavily at the foot of the ramp, dropped her face into her hands. Feya nodded again, swallowing.

"She gave orders that the northern and western borders were to be guarded against the High One's harpist, that no one in Herun should give him lodgings or aid of any kind, and that anyone seeing him in Herun should tell either the guards or the Morgol. And she told us why. She sent messengers to all parts of Herun to tell people. And then she left."

Lyra's gaze moved from her, past the worn, grey clutter of warehouse roofs lining the docks, to the border hills touched to a transient, delicate green under the late spring sun. She whispered, "Deth."

Trika cleared her throat. "We thought she might have gone to look for him. Lyra, I don't—none of us understand how he could have done the terrible thing the Star-Bearer accused him of; how he could have lied to the Morgol. It doesn't seem possible. How could—how could he not love the Morgol?"

"Maybe he does," Lyra said slowly. She caught Raederle's quick glance and added defensively, "She judged him like Danan, like Har: without even listening to him, without giving him the right to self-defense that she would give to the simplest man from the Herun marsh towns."

"I don't understand him either," Raederle said steadily. "But he admitted his guilt when I talked to him. And he offered no defense. He had none."

"It doesn't seem to have occurred to anyone, even Morgon, that perhaps Ghisteslwchlohm held Deth in his power, as he held the wizards, and forced him to bring Morgon to him instead of to the High One."

"Lyra, Ghisteslwchlohm is—" She stopped, felt the sluice of the sea wind between them like an impossible distance. She sensed their waiting, and finished wearily, "You're saying that the Founder is more powerful than the High One, forcing his harpist against his will. And if there is one thing I believe about Deth, it is that no one, maybe not even the High One, could force him to do something he did not choose to do."

"Then you've condemned him, too," Lyra said flatly.

"He condemned himself! Do you think I want to

believe it, either? He lied to everyone, he betrayed the Star-Bearer, the Morgol and the High One. And he put his cloak over me so that I wouldn't be cold while I slept, that night in the backlands. That's all I know." She met Lyra's dark, brooding gaze helplessly. "Ask him. That's what you want, isn't it? Find him and ask him. You know where he is: in the backlands, heading toward Lungold. And you know that must be where the Morgol is going."

Lyra was silent. She dropped down on the ramp beside Tristan, yielding to a weary, vulnerable uncertainty.

Goh said simply after a moment, "We have no instructions from the Morgol to stay in Herun. No one should travel in the backlands alone."

"I wonder if she looked beyond Herun and saw him alone . . ." She took a breath impulsively, as though to give an order, then closed her mouth abruptly.

Trika said soberly, "Lyra, none of us knows what to do; we have no orders. It would be a relief to us all if you postponed resigning for a while."

"All right. Saddle your horses and let's go to Crown City. No matter how secretly she rode out of Herun, even the Morgol must have left some kind of trail."

The guards dispersed. Raederle sat down beside Lyra. They were silent as a sailor tramped down the ramp, leading Lyra's horse and whistling softly.

Lyra, her spear slanted on her knees, said suddenly to Raederle, "Do you think I'm right in following her?"

Raederle nodded. She remembered the worn, familiar face of the harpist, etched in the firelight with an unfamiliar mockery as he drank, the light irony in his voice that had never been there before. She whispered, "Yes. She'll need you."

"What will you do? Will you come?"

"No. I'll sail back to Caithnard with Bri. If Morgon is heading south, he might go there."

Lyra glanced at her. "He'll go to An."

"Maybe."

"And then where will he go? Lungold?"

"I don't know. Wherever Deth is, I suppose."

On the other side of Lyra, Tristan lifted her head. "Do you think," she said with unexpected bitterness, "that he'll come to Hed before that? Or is he planning to kill Deth and then go home and tell everyone about it?"

They looked at her. Her eyes were heavy with unshed tears; her mouth was pinched taut. She added after a moment, staring down at the bolt heads in the planks, "If he wouldn't move so fast, if I could just catch up with him, maybe I could persuade him to come home. But how can I do that if he won't stay still?"

"He'll go home eventually," Raederle said. "I can't believe he's changed so much he doesn't care about Hed any more."

"He's changed. Once he was the land-ruler of Hed, and he would rather have killed himself than someone else. Now—"

"Tristan, he has been hurt, probably more deeply than any of us could know . . ."

She nodded a little jerkily. "I can understand that with my head. People have killed other people in Hed, out of anger or jealousy, but not—not like that. Not tracking someone like a hunter, driving him to one certain place to be killed. It's—what someone else would do. But not Morgon. And if— if it happens, and afterwards he goes back to Hed, how will we recognize each other any more?"

They were silent. A sailor carrying a keg of wine across his shoulders shook the ramp with his slow, heavy, persistent steps. Behind them, Bri

Corbett shouted something, lost like a sea gull's cry in the wind. Raederle stirred.

"He'll know that," she said softly. "Deep in him. That he has every justification to do this except one. That the only man who might condemn him for it would be himself. Maybe you should trust him a little. Go home and wait and trust him."

There was another step behind them. Bri Corbett said, looking down at them, "That is the most rational thing I've heard this entire journey. Who's for home?"

"Caithnard," Raederle said, and he sighed.

"Well, it's close enough for a start. Maybe I can look for work there, if your father decides he doesn't want to see my face in An after this. But if I can just get you and this ship together back into the harbor at Anuin, he can curse the hair off my head and I'll still be content."

Lyra stood up. She hugged Bri suddenly, upsetting his hat with her spearhead. "Thank you. Tell Mathom it was my fault."

He straightened his hat, his face flushed, smiling. "I doubt if he'd be impressed."

"Have you heard any news of him here?" Raederle asked. "Is he back home?"

"No one seems to know. But—" He stopped, his brows tugging together, and she nodded.

"It's been nearly two months. He doesn't have a vow to fulfill anymore, since Morgon is alive, and he won't have a house to return to if he doesn't get himself back to An before it rouses." The guards rounded the dock side, in two straight lines. Kia, holding Lyra's horse, brought it over to her. Raederle and Tristan stood up, and Lyra gave them her quick, taut embrace.

"Good-bye. Go home." She held Raederle's eyes

a moment before she loosed her and repeated softly, "Go home."

She turned, mounted, and gave them a spear-bearer's salute, her spear flaring upward like a silver torch. Then she wheeled her horse, took her place beside Trika at the head of the lines, and led the guards out of the Hlurle docks without looking back. Raederle watched her until the last guard disappeared behind the warehouses. Then she turned almost aimlessly and saw the empty ramp before her. She went up slowly, found Bri and Tristan watching the flicker of spears in the distance. Bri sighed.

"It's going to be a quiet journey without some-one using the boom for target practice. We'll finish getting supplies here and sail a straight run past Ymris to Caithnard. Making," he added grimly, "the widest possible detour around Ymris. I would rather see the King of An himself off my bowsprit than Astrin Ymris."

They saw neither on the long journey to Caith-nard, only an occasional trade-ship making its own prudent path around the troubled Ymris coast. Sometimes the ships drew near to exchange news, for tales of the errant ship out of An had spread from one end of the realm to the other. The news was always the same: war in Ymris had spread up into Tor and east Umber; no one knew where Morgon was; no one had heard anything of Mathom of An; and one startling piece of news from Caithnard: the ancient College of Riddle-Masters had sent away its students and closed its doors.

The long journey ended finally as the weary ship took the lolling afternoon tide into the Caithnard harbor. There were cheers and various remarks from the dockside as the dark sails wrinkled and slumped on the mast and Bri eased the ship into its berth. Bri ignored the noise with patience tempered by experience, and said to Raederle, "We're taking in a little water; she'll need repairs and supplies before we continue to Anuin. It will be a day or two, maybe. Do you want me to find you lodgings in the city?"

"It doesn't matter." She gathered her thoughts with an effort. "Yes. Please. I'll need my horse."

"All right."

Tristan cleared her throat. "And I'll need mine."

"You will." He eyed her. "For what? Riding across the water to Hed?"

"I'm not going to Hed, I've decided." She bore up steadily under his flat gaze. "I'm going to that city—the wizards' city. Lungold. I know where it is; I've looked on your maps. The road leads straight out of—"

"Hegdis-Noon's curved eyeteeth, girl, have you got a sensible bone anywhere in you?" Bri exploded. "That's a six-weeks journey through no-man's land. It's only because I have a hold weeping bilge water that I didn't take you straight to Tol. Lungold! With Deth and Morgon headed there, the Founder and who knows how many wizards coming like wraiths out of the barrows of Hel, that city is going to fall apart like a worm-eaten hull."

"I don't care. I—"

"You—"

They both stopped, as Tristan, her eyes moving past Bri, took a step backward. Raederle turned. A young man with a dark, tired, vaguely familiar face had come up the ramp. Something in his plain dress, his hesitant entry onto Bri's ship, stirred a memory in her mind. His eyes went to her face as she moved, and then, beyond her, to Tristan.

He stopped, closing his eyes, and sighed. Then he said, "Tristan, will you please come home before Eliard leaves Hed to look for you."

Something of the mutinous, trapped expression in her eyes faded. "He wouldn't."

"He would. He will. A trader coming down from Kraal spotted this ship at Hlurle and said you were coming south. Eliard was ready to leave then, but we—I won a wrestling match with him, and he said if I came back without you, he'd leave Hed. He's worn to the bone with worry, and his temper is short as a hen's nose. There's no living on the same island with him, drunk or sober."

"Cannon, I want to come home, but—"

Cannon Master shifted his stance on the deck. "Let me put it this way. I have asked you politely, and I will ask you again. The third time, I won't ask."

Tristan gazed at him, her chin lifted. Bri Corbett allowed a slow smile of pure contentment to spread over his face. Tristan opened her mouth to retort; then, under the weight of Cannon's implacable, harassed gaze, changed tactics visibly.

"Cannon, I know where Morgon is, or where he's going to be. If you'll just wait, just tell Eliard to wait—"

"Tell him. I told him it was a fine morning once and he threw a bucket of slops at me. Face one thing, Tristan: when Morgon wants to come home, he'll come. Without help from any of us. Just as he managed to survive. I'm sure, by now, he appreciates the fact that you cared enough to try to find out what happened to him."

"You could come with me—"

"It takes all my courage just to stand here with that bottomless water between me and Hed. If you want him to come home, then go back yourself. In the High One's name, give him something he loves to come home to."

Tristan was silent, while the water murmured against the hull and the lean black shadow of the mast lay like a bar at her feet. She said finally, "All right," and took a step forward. She stopped. "I'll go home and tell Eliard I'm all right. But I don't promise to stay. I don't promise that." She took another step, then turned to Raederle and held her tightly. "Be careful," she said softly. "And if you see Morgon, tell him . . . Just tell him that. And tell him to come home."

She loosed Raederle, went slowly to Cannon's side. He dropped a hand down her hair, drew her against him, and after a moment she slid an arm around his waist. Raederle watched them go down the ramp, make their way through the hectic, disorderly docks. A longing for Anuin wrenched at her, for Duac, and Elieu of Hel, for Rood with his crow-sharp eyes, for the sounds and smells of An, sun-spiced oak and the whisper, deep in the earth, of the endless fabric of history.

Bri Corbett said gently behind her, "Don't be sad. You'll smell the wind of your own home in a week."

"Will I?" She looked down and saw the white brand on her palm that had nothing to do with An. Then sensing the worry in him, she added more lightly, "I need to get off this ship, I think. Will you ask them to bring my horse up?"

"If you'll wait, I'll escort you."

She put a hand on his shoulder. "I'll be all right. I want to be alone for a while."

She rode through the docks, down the busy merchants' streets of the city, and if anyone troubled her, she did not notice. The fading afternoon drew a net of shadows across her path as she turned onto the silent road that led up to the College. She realized she had seen no students that day, with their bright robes and restless minds, anywhere in Caithnard. There were none on the road. She took the final wind to the top and saw the empty sweep of the College grounds.

She stopped. The dark, ancient stones with their blank windows seemed to house a hollowness, a betrayal of truth as bitter and terrible as the betrayal at Erlenstar Mountain. The shadow of that mountain had swept across the realm into the hearts of the Masters, until they found the greatest deceit within their own walls. They could send the students away, but she knew that though they might question themselves, they would never question the constant, essential weave and patterning of Riddle-Mastery.

She dismounted at the door and knocked. No one came, so she opened it. The narrow hall was empty, dark. She walked down it slowly, glimpsing through the long line of open doors each small chamber that had once held bed, books and endless games over guttering candles. There was no one downstairs. She took the broad stone stairs to the second floor and found more lines of open doors, the rooms holding no more in them than an expressionless block of sky. She came finally to the door of the Masters' library. It was closed.

She opened it. Eight Masters and a King, interrupting their quiet discussion, turned to her, startled. The King's eyes, ancient, ice-blue, burned as he looked at her with sudden curiosity.

One of the Masters rose. He said gently, "Raederle of An. Is there some way we can help you?"

"I hope so," she whispered, "because I have no place else to go."

8

SHE TOLD THEM, SITTING IN THEIR GENTLE, IM-
partial silence, of the shape-changer, who had
come to her in Danan's house, and of her flight
out of Isig Mountain. She told them of the stone
Astrin had found on King's Mouth Plain and
showed them the mark of it on her palm. She told
them how she had held fire in the empty hollow of
night in the backlands, while the wine cup of the
High One's harpist flashed and fell in its light. She
told them, knowing they knew it, but telling them
by right of sorrow and heritage, the tale of Ylon,
born out of An and the formless sea, and she saw
in their eyes the gathering of the threads of riddlery. When she finished, dusk had crept in to the
room, blurring the silent, dark-robed figures, old
parchment and priceless, gold-hinged manuscripts.
One of the Masters lit a candle. The flame gave
her the patient, weary working of lines on his face,
and beyond him, the spare, ungentle face of the
Osterland King. The Master said simply, "We are
all questioning ourselves these days."

"I know. I know how imperatively. You have
not closed your doors only because you accepted

the Founder of Lungold as a Master here. I know who was there to meet Morgon when Deth brought him to Erlenstar Mountain."

The taper the Master held dipped toward a wick and halted. "You know that, too."

"I guessed. And later, Deth—Deth told me it was so."

"He seems to have spared you very little," Har said. His voice sounded dry, impersonal, but she saw in his face a hint of the anger and confusion the harpist had loosed into the realm.

"I was not asking to be spared. I wanted truth. I want it now, so I came here. It's a place to start from. I can't go back to An with this. If my father were there, maybe I could. But I can't go back and pretend to Duac and Rood and the Lords of An that I belong to An as surely as the roots of trees and the old barrows of Kings. I have power, and I am afraid of it. I don't know—I don't know what I might loose in myself without meaning to. I don't know, any more, where I belong. I don't know what to do."

"Ignorance," the wolf-king murmured, "is deadly."

Master Tel shifted, his worn robe rustling in the hush. "You both came for answers; we have few to give you. Sometimes, however, the turn of a question becomes an answer; and we do have many questions. Above all: one regarding the shape-changers. They appeared almost without warning at the moment the Star-Bearer began realizing his destiny. They knew his name before he did; they knew of the sword bearing his stars deep in the grave of the Earth-Masters' children at Isig. They are old, older than the first weave of history and riddlery, originless, unnamed. They must be named. Only then will you know the origins of your own power."

"What else do I need to know about them, except that they have tried to destroy the King's lines in An and Ymris, that they blinded Astrin, they almost killed Morgon, they have no mercy, no pity, no love. They gave Ylon his life, then drove him to his death. They have no compassion even for their own—" She stopped, then, remembering the voice of the shape-changer striking its unexpected, puzzling timbre of richness.

One of the Masters said softly, "You have touched an incongruity?"

"Not compassion, but passion . . ." she whispered. "The shape-changer answered me with that. And then she wove her fire into such beauty that I hungered for her power. And she asked me what had driven Ylon back to them, if they were so terrible. She made me hear the harping Ylon heard, made me understand his longing. Then she told me Morgon had killed the harpist." She paused in their silence, the practiced stillness of old men, the heart of patience. "She handed me that riddle." Her voice was toneless. "That incongruity. Like Deth's kindness, which maybe was only habit, and . . . maybe not. I don't know. Nothing—the High One, this College, good or evil—seems to keep its own shape any more. That's why I wanted Morgon, then, so badly. At least he knows his own name. And a man who can name himself can see to name other things."

Their faces under the restless candlelight seemed molded out of shadow and memory, they sat so quietly when her voice faded.

At last Master Tel said gently, "Things are themselves. We twist the shapes of them. Your own name lies within you still, a riddle. The High One, whoever he is, is still the High One, though Ghisteslwchlohm has worn his name like a mask."

"And the High One's harpist is what?" Har

asked. Master Tel was silent a moment, with-drawing into a memory.

"He studied here, also, centuries ago ... I would not have believed a man who took the Black could have so betrayed the disciplines of riddle-mastery."

"Morgon intends to kill him," Har said brusquely, and the Master's eyes lifted again, startled.

"I had not heard ..."

"Is that a betrayal of riddle-mastery? The wise man does not pursue his own shadow. There are no instincts of his own land-law in him to stay his hand; there is not one land-ruler, including the Morgol, who will not comply with his wishes. We give him understanding; we bar the gates to our kingdoms as he requests. And we wait for his final betrayal: self-betrayal." His implacable gaze moved from face to face like a challenge. "The Master is master of himself. Morgon has absolute freedom of this realm. He has no longer the re-straints of land-law. The High One is nowhere in evidence except in the evidence of his existence. Morgon has bound himself, so far, to his destiny by the tenets of riddle-mastery. He also has enor-mous, untested power. Is there a riddle on the master lists that permits the wise man to revenge?"

"Judgment," one of the Masters murmured, but his eyes were troubled. "Who else is permitted to judge and condemn this man who has betrayed the entire realm for centuries?"

"The High One."

"In lieu of the High One—"

"The Star-Bearer?" He twisted their silence like a harp string, then broke it. "The man who wrested his power from Ghisteslwchlohm because no one, not even the High One, gave him any help? He is bitter, self-sufficient, and by his actions he is ques-tioning even the elusive restraints of riddle-mastery. But I doubt if he sees even that in himself, because wherever he looks there is Deth. His destiny is to answer riddles. Not destroy them."

Something eased in Raederle's mind. She said softly, "Did you tell him that?"

"I tried."

"You complied with his wishes. Deth said he was driven out of Osterland by your wolves."

"I had no desire to find even the shape of Deth's footprint in my land." He paused; his voice lost its harshness. "When I saw the Star-Bearer, I would have given him the scars off my hands. He said very little about Deth or even about Ghisteslwchlohm, but he said . . . enough. Later, as I began to realize what he was doing, how far from himself he seemed to have grown, the implications of his actions haunted me. He was always so stubborn . . ."

"Is he coming to Caithnard?"

"No. He asked me to take his tale and his riddles to the Masters, who in their wisdom would decide whether or not the realm could bear the truth about the one we have called the High One for so long."

"That's why you shut your doors," she said suddenly to Master Tel, and he nodded, with the first trace of weariness she had ever seen in him.

"How can we call ourselves Masters?" he asked simply. "We have withdrawn into ourselves not out of horror, but out of a need to reconstruct the patterns we have called truth. In the very fabric of the realm, its settlement, histories, tales, wars, poetry, its riddles—if there is an answer there, a shape of truth that holds to itself, we will find it. If the tenets of riddle-mastery themselves are invalid, we will find that, too. The Master of Hed, in his actions, will tell us that."

"He found his way out of that dark tower in Aum . . ." she murmured. Har shifted.

"Do you think he can find his way out of another tower, another deadly game? This time, he has what he always wanted: choice. The power to make his own rules for the game."

She thought of the cold, sagging tower in Aum, rising like a solitary riddle itself among the gold-green oak, and saw a young man, simply dressed, stand in front of the worm-eaten door in the sunlight a long time before he moved. Then he lifted a hand, pushed the door open, and disappeared, leaving the soft air and the sunlight behind him. She looked at Har, feeling as though he had asked her a riddle and something vital hung balanced on her simple answer. She said, "Yes," and knew that the answer had come from someplace beyond all uncertainty and confusion, beyond logic.

He was silent a moment, studying her. Then he said, his voice gentle as the mill of snow through the still, misty air of his land, "Morgon told me once that he sat alone in an old inn at Hlurle, midway on his journey to Erlenstar Mountain, and waited for a ship to take him back to Hed. That was one point when he felt he had a choice about the matter of his destiny. But one thing stopped him from going home: the knowledge that he could never ask you to come to Hed if he could not give you the truth of his own name, of himself. So he finished his journey. When I saw him come into my house not long ago, as simply as any traveller seeking shelter in my house from the night, I did not at first see the Star-Bearer. I saw only the terrible, relentless patience in a man's eyes: the patience born out of absolute loneliness. He went into a dark tower of truth for you. Do you have the courage to give him your own name?"

Her hands closed tightly, one clenched over the pattern of angles on her palm. She felt something in her that had been knotted like a fist ease open slowly. She nodded, not trusting her voice, and her hand opened, glinting with secret knowledge in the candlelight. "Yes," she said then. "Whatever I have of Ylon's power, I swear by my name, I will twist it beyond possibility into something of value. Where is he?"

"Coming through Ymris, undoubtedly, on his way to Anuin, and then to Lungold, since that seems to be where he is forcing Deth to go."

"And then where? After that, where? He will not be able to go back to Hed."

"No. Not if he kills the harpist. There would be no peace for him in Hed. I don't know. Where does a man go to escape from himself? I'll ask him that when I see him in Lungold."

"You're going there—"

He nodded. "I thought he might need one friend in Lungold."

"Please, I want to come with you."

She saw the unspoken protest in the Masters' faces. The wolf-king flicked a thin brow. "How far will you go to escape from yourself? Lungold? And then where? How far can a tree escape from its roots?"

"I'm not trying to—" She stopped then, not looking at him.

He said softly, "Go home."

"Har," Master Tel said somberly, "that is advice you might well give yourself. That city is no place even for you. The wizards will seek Ghistesl-wchlohm there; the Star-Bearer will seek Deth; and if the shape-changers gather there also, not a living thing in that city will be safe."

"I know," Har said, and the smile deepened faintly in his eyes. "There were traders in Kraal when I passed through it, who asked me where I thought the wizards had gone when they vanished. They were men who used both eyes to see out of, and they could look across half the realm to wonder if they wanted to risk their lives trading in a doomed city. Traders, like animals, have an instinct for danger."

"So do you," Master Tel said, with some severity, "but without the instinct to avoid it."

"Where do you suggest we go to be safe in a doomed realm? And when, in the void between a riddle and its answer, was there ever anything but danger?"

Master Tel shook his head. He yielded the argument finally when he realized it had become one-sided. They rose then for supper, cooked for them by a handful of students who had no other family but the Masters, no home but the College. They spent the rest of the evening in the library, while Raederle and the wolf-king listened, discussing the possible origins of the shape-changers, the implications of the stone found on King's Mouth Plain, and the strange face within it.

"The High One?" Master Tel suggested at one point, and Raederle's throat closed in a nameless fear. "Is it possible they could be so interested in finding him?"

"Why should they be any more interested in the High One than he is in them?"

"Perhaps the High One is hiding from them," someone else suggested. Har, sitting so quietly in the shadows Raederle had almost forgotten him, lifted his head suddenly, but he said nothing. One of the other Masters picked up the weave of the thought.

"If the High One lived in fear of them, why wouldn't Ghisteslwchlohm? The law of the High One in the realm has been untroubled; he seems oblivious of them, rather than frightened. And yet . . . he is an Earth-Master; Morgon's stars are inextricably bound to the earlier doom of the Earth-

Masters and their children; it seems incredible that he has made no response to this threat to his realm."

"What precisely is the threat? What are the extent of their powers? What are their origins? Who are they? What do they want? What does Ghisteslwchlohm want? Where is the High One?"

The questions spun into a haze like torch smoke in the room; massive books were drawn from the shelves, pored over, left lying with wax from the candles pooling in their margins. Raederle saw the various unlockings of wizards' books, heard the names or phrases that opened the seamless bindings of iron or brass or gold; saw the black, hurried writing that never faded, the blank pages that revealed their writings like an eye slowly opening to the touch of water, or fire, or a line of irrelevant poetry. Finally the broad tables were hidden beneath books, dusty rolls of parchment, and guttered candles; and unanswered riddles seemed to be burning on the wicks, lying in the shadows of the chair-backs and bookshelves. The Masters fell silent. Raederle, struggling with weariness, thought she could still hear their voices or their thoughts converging and separating, questioning, discarding, beyond the silence. Then Har rose a little stiffly, went to one of the books lying open and turned a page. "There is an old tale nagging at my mind that may not be worth considering: one out of Ymris, in Aloil's collection of legends, I think, with a suggestion of shape-changing in it . . ."

Raederle stood up, feeling the fraying tendrils of thought stir and eddy around her. The Masters' faces seemed remote, vaguely surprised as she moved. She said apologetically, "I'm half-asleep."

"I'm sorry," Master Tel said. He put a gentle hand on her arm, led her to the door. "One of the students had the forethought and kindness to go to the docks and tell your ship-master you were here; he brought your pack back with him. There will be a room prepared somewhere; I'm not sure—"

He opened the door, and a young student lounging beside the wall, reading, straightened abruptly and closed his book. He had a lean, dark, hook-nosed face, and a shy smile, with which he greeted Raederle. He still wore the robe of his rank: Beginning Mastery; the long sleeves were stained at the hems as though he had helped cook supper in it. He ducked his head after he gave her the smile and said diffidently to the floor, "We made a bed for you near the Masters' chambers. I brought your things."

"Thank you." She said good-night to Master Tel and followed the young student through the quiet halls. He said nothing more, his head still bent, the flush of shyness in his cheeks. He led her into one of the small, bare chambers. Her pack lay on the bed; pitchers of water and wine stood on a tiny table under a branch of burning candles. The windows, inset deeply in the rough stone, were open to the dark, salty air billowing up over the cliff's edge. She said, "Thank you," again and went to look out, though she could see nothing but the old moon with a lost star drifting between its horns. She heard the student take an uncertain step behind her.

"The sheets are rough . . ." Then he closed the door and said, "Raederle."

Her blood froze in her veins.

In the soft, shifting light of the candles, his face was a blur of spare lines and shadows. He was taller than she remembered; the stained white robe that had not changed with his shape-changing was puckered and strained across his shoulders. A wind shift stirred the candlelight, pulled the flames toward him and she saw his eyes. She put her hands to her mouth.

"Morgon?" Her voice jumped uncontrollably. Neither of them moved; a solid slab of air seemed wedged like stone between them. He looked at her out of eyes that had stared endlessly into the black, inner hollows of Erlenstar Mountain, into the rifts and hollows of a wizard's brain. Then she moved forward, through the stone, touched and held something that seemed ageless, like the wind or night, of every shape and no shape, as worn as a pebble runnelled with water, tossed for an eon at the bottom of a mountain. He moved slightly, and the knowledge of his own shape returned to her hands. She felt his hand, light as a breath, stir her hair. Then they were apart again, though she did not know which one of them had moved.

"I would have come to you at Anuin, but you were here." His voice sounded deep, harrowed, over-used. He moved finally, sat down on the bed. She stared at him wordlessly. He met her eyes, and his face, a stranger's face, lean, hard-boned, still, shaded into a sudden, haunting gentleness. "I didn't mean to frighten you."

"You didn't." Her own voice sounded remote in her ears, as though it were the wind beside her speaking. She sat down beside him. "I've been looking for you."

"I know. I heard."

"I didn't think . . . Har said you weren't coming here."

"I saw your father's ship off the coasts of Ymris. I thought, since Tristan was with you, it might stop here. So I came."

"She might still be here; Cannon Master came for her, but—"

"They've gone to Hed."

The finality in his voice made her study him a moment. "You don't want to see her."

"Not yet."

"She asked me, if I saw you, to tell you this: be careful."

He was silent, still meeting her eyes. He had, she realized slowly, a gift for silence. When he chose, it seemed to ebb out of him, the worn silence of old trees or stones lying motionless for years. It was measured to his breathing, in his motionless, scarred hands. He moved abruptly, soundlessly, and it flowed with him as he turned, stood where she had been, gazing out the window. She wondered briefly if he could see Hed in the night.

"I heard tales of your journey," he said. "Tristan, Lyra and you together on Mathom's ship stealing by night out of Caithnard, blinding seven Ymris war-ships with a light like a small sun, taking a slow barge up the floodwaters of the Winter to the doorstep of the High One to ask him a question . . . And you tell me to be careful. What was that light that blinded even Astrin? It gave rise, among the traders, to marvellous speculation. Even I was curious."

She started to answer him, then stopped. "What conclusions did you come to?"

He turned, came back to her side again. "That it was something you did, probably. I remembered you could do small things . . ."

"Morgon—"

"Wait. I'll want to tell you now that—no matter what else has happened or will happen—it mattered to me that while I was coming down from Isig, you were making that journey. I heard your name, now and then, as I moved, Lyra's, Tristan's, like small, distant lights, unexpectedly."

"She wanted to see you so badly. Couldn't you have—"

"Not yet."

"Then when?" she said helplessly. "After you've killed Deth? Morgon, that will be one harpist too many."

His face did not change, but his eyes slid away from her, towards some memory. "Corrig?" He added after a moment, "I had forgotten him."

She swallowed, feeling as though the simple statement had set the slab of distance between them again. He assumed his stillness like a shield, impervious and impenetrable; she wondered if it hid a total stranger or someone as familiar to her as his name. He seemed, looking at her, to read her thoughts. He reached across the distance, touched her briefly. Then another memory, shapeless, terrible, welled through the stillness into his eyes; he turned his face slightly until it faded. He said softly, "I should have waited to see you, too. But I just—I wanted to look at something very beautiful. The legend of An. The great treasure of the Three Portions. To know that you still exist. I needed that."

His fingers brushed her again, as though she were something fragile as a moth wing. She closed her eyes, brought the heels of her hands against them and whispered, "Oh, Morgon. What in Hel's name do you think I'm doing in this College?" She let her hands fall and wondered if, behind the armor of his solitude, she had at last got his attention. "I would be that for you, if I could," she cried. "I would be mute, beautiful, changeless as the earth of An for you. I would be your memory, without age, always innocent, always waiting in the King's white house at Anuin—I would do that for you and for no other man in the realm. But it would be a lie, and I will do anything but lie to

you—I swear that. A riddle is a tale so familiar
you no longer see it; it's simply there, like the air
you breathe, the ancient names of Kings echoing
in the corners of your house, the sunlight in the
corner of your eye; until one day you look at it
and something shapeless, voiceless in you opens
a third eye and sees it as you have never seen it
before. Then you are left with the knowledge of
the nameless question in you, and the tale that is
no longer meaningless but the one thing in the
world that has meaning any more." She stopped
for breath; his hand had closed without gentleness,
around her wrist. His face was familiar finally,
questioning, uncertain.

"What riddle? You came here, to this place,
with a riddle?"

"Where else could I go? My father was gone; I
tried to find you and I couldn't. You should have
known there was nothing in the world that would
not change—"

"What riddle?"

"You're the Master here; do I have to tell even
you?"

His hand tightened. "No," he said, and applied
himself in silence to one final game within those
walls. She waited, her own mind working the riddle with him, setting her name against her life,
against the history of An, following strand after
strand of thought that led nowhere, until at last he
touched one possibility that built evenly onto another and onto another. She felt his fingers shift.
Then his head lifted slowly, until he met her eyes
again and she wished that the College would dis-
solve into the sea.

"Ylon." He let the word wear away into another
silence. "I never saw it. It was always there . . ."
He loosed her abruptly, rose and spat an ancient
curse on a single tone into the shadows. It pat-

terned the glass in the window with cracks like a spider's web. "They touched even you."

She stared numbly at the place where his hand had been. She rose to leave, not knowing where in the world she could go. He caught her in one step, turned her to face him.

"Do you think I care?" he demanded incredulously. "Do you think that? Who am I to judge you? I am so blind with hatred I can't even see my own land or the people I loved once. I'm hunting a man who never carried weapons in his life, to kill him while he stands facing me, against the advice of every land-ruler I have spoken to. What have you ever done in your life to make me have anything but respect for you?"

"I've never done anything in my life."

"You gave me truth."

She was silent, in the hard grip of his hands, seeing his face beyond its husk of stillness—bitter, vulnerable, lawless—the brand of stars on his forehead beneath his dishevelled hair. Her own hands lifted, closed on his arms. She whispered, "Morgon, be careful."

"Of what? For what? Do you know who was there in Erlenstar Mountain to meet me that day Deth brought me there?"

"Yes. I guessed."

"The Founder of Lungold has been sitting at the apex of the world for centuries, dispensing justice in the name of the High One. Where can I go to demand justice? That harpist is landless, bound to no King's law; the High One seems oblivious to both our fates. Will anyone care if I kill him? In Ymris, in An itself, no one would question it—"

"No one will ever question anything you do! You are your own law, your own justice! Danan, Har, Heureu, the Morgol—they will give you everything you ask for the sake of your name, and the truth you

163

have borne alone; but Morgon, if you create your own law, where will any of us go, if we ever need to, to demand retribution from you?"

He gazed down at her; she saw the flick of uncertainty in his eyes. Then his head shook, slowly, stubbornly. "Just one thing. Just this one thing. Someone will kill him eventually—a wizard, perhaps Ghisteslwchlohm himself. And I have the right."

"Morgon—"

His hands tightened painfully. He was no longer seeing her but some black, private horror in his memory. She saw the sweat bead at his hairline, the muscles jump in his rigid face. He whispered, "While Ghisteslwchlohm was in my mind, nothing else existed. But at times when he . . . when he left me and I found myself still alive, lying in the dark, empty caverns of Erlenstar, I could hear Deth playing. Sometimes he played songs from Hed. He gave me something to live for."

She closed her eyes. The harpist's elusive face rose in her mind, blurred away; she felt the hard, twisted knot of Morgon's bewildered rage and the harpist's deceit like an unending, unanswerable riddle that no stricture could justify, and no Master in his quiet library could unravel. His torment ached in her; his loneliness seemed a vast hollow into which words would drop and disappear like pebbles. She understood then how his briefest word had closed court after court, kingdom after kingdom as he made his difficult, secret path through the realm. She whispered Har's words, "I would give you the scars off my hands." His hold loosened finally. He looked down at her a long time before he spoke.

"But you will not allow me that one right."

She shook her head; her voice came with effort. "You'll kill him, but even dead he'll eat at your heart until you understand him."

His hands dropped. He turned away from her,

went again to the window. He touched the glass he had cracked, then turned again abruptly. She could barely see his face in the shadows; his voice sounded rough.

"I have to leave. I don't know when I will see you again."

"Where are you going?"

"Anuin. To speak to Duac. I'll be gone before you ever reach it. It's best that way, for both of us. If Ghisteslwchlohm ever realized how he could use you, I would be helpless; I would give him my heart with both my hands if he asked."

"And then where?"

"To find Deth. And then, I don't—" He checked abruptly. The silence eddied about him again as he stood listening; he seemed to blur at the edge of the candlelight. She listened, heard nothing but the night wind among the shivering flames, the wordless riddling of the sea. She took a step toward him.

"Is it Ghisteslwchlohm?" Her voice was muted to his stillness. He did not answer, and she could not tell if he had heard her. A fear beat suddenly in the back of her throat; she whispered, "Morgon." His face turned towards her then. She heard the sudden, dry catch of his breath. But he did not move until she went to him. Then he gathered her slowly, wearily into his silence, his face dropping against her hair.

"I have to go. I'll come to you at Anuin. For judgment."

"No—"

He shook his head slightly, stilling her. She felt, as her hands slid away from him, the strange, almost formless tension of air where he might have slung a sword beneath his robe. He said something she could not hear, his voice matching the wind's murmur. She saw a flame-streaked shadow and then a memory.

She undressed, lay awake for a long time before she finally fell into a troubled sleep. She woke hours later, stared, startled, into the darkness. Thoughts were crowding into her mind, a tumultuous cross-weave of names, longings, memories, anger, a spattering cauldron of events, urges, inarticulate voices. She sat up, wondering what shape-changer's mind she had become embroiled in, but there was an odd recognition in her that had nothing to do with them, that turned her face unerringly towards An, as if she could see it through the blank stone walls and the night. She felt her heart begin to pound. Roots tugged at her; her heritage of grass-molded barrows, rotting towers, kings' names, wars and legends, pulling her towards a chaos the earth, left lawless too long, was slowly unleashing. She stood up, her hands sliding over her mouth, realizing two things at once. The whole of An was rousing at last. And the Star-Bearer's path would lead him straight into Hel.

9

SHE RODE OUT OF CAITHNARD AT DAWN, STOOD A day and a half later in the vast oak forest bordering Hel, straining, as she had never done before, to unlock all the power and awareness in her mind. She had already sensed, as she came through the forest, the almost imperceptible movement of someone ahead of her, his need like a faint, indistinguishable scent, for swiftness, for secrecy. And at night, sleepless and aware, she had glimpsed for one terrifying moment, like the shape of some enormous beast rising against the moonlight, a relentless, powerful, enraged mind focussed to a single thought of destruction.

She wondered, as she stood looking over Hallard Blackdawn's lands, what shape Morgon was taking through them. The pastures, sloping gently towards the river that ran beside the Lord's house, looked quiet enough, but there was not an animal on them. She could hear hounds baying in the distance, wild, hoarse keening that never seemed to stop. There were no men working in the fields behind the house, and she was not surprised. That corner of Hel had been the last battlefield in the half-forgotten wars between Hel and An; it had held its own in an endless series of fierce, desperate battles until Oen of An, sweeping through Aum six centuries earlier, had almost contemptuously smashed the last stronghold of resistance and beheaded the last of the Kings of Hel, who had taken refuge there. The land had always been uneasy with legend; the turn of a plow could still unearth an ancient sword eaten to the core with age or the shaft of a broken spear banded with rings of gold. In so many centuries, King Farr of Hel, bereft of his head, had had much leisure to ponder his grievances, and, loosed at last from the earth, he would have wasted little time gathering himself out of Hallard's fields. The chaos of voices Raederle had heard two nights earlier had faded into a frightening stillness: the dead were unbound, aware, and plotting.

She saw, as she rode across Hallard's upper pastures, a group of riders swing out of the woods into a meadow across her path. She reined, her heart pounding, then recognized the broad, black-haired figure of Hallard Blackdawn towering above his men. They were armed, but lightly; there was a suggestion of futility in their bare heads and the short swords at their sides. She sensed, unexpectedly, their exasperation and uncertainty. Hallard's head turned as she sat watching; she could not see his eyes, but she felt the startled leap in his mind of her name.

She lifted the reins in her hands hesitantly as he galloped up to her. She had no desire to argue with him, but she needed news. So she did not move, and he pulled up in front of her, big-boned, dark, sweating in the hot, silent afternoon. He groped for words a moment, then said explosively, "Someone should flay that ship-master. After taking you to Isig and back, he let you ride unescorted from Caithnard into this? Have you had news of your father?"

She shook her head. "Nothing. Is it bad?"

"Bad." He closed his eyes. "Those hounds have been at it for two solid days. Half my livestock is missing; my wheat fields look as though they've been harrowed by millwheels, and the ancient barrows in the south fields have been flattened to the ground by nothing human." He opened his eyes again; they were red-veined with lack of sleep. "I don't know what it's like in the rest of An. I sent a messenger to east Aum yesterday, to Cyn Croeg. He couldn't even get across the border. He came back babbling of whispering trees. I sent another to Anuin; I don't know if he'll make it. And if he does, what can Duac do? What can you do against the dead?" He waited, pleading for an answer, then shook his head. "Curse your father," he said bluntly. "He'll have to fight Oen's wars over again if he isn't careful. I'd wrest kingship from the land myself, if I could think how."

"Well," she said, "maybe that's what they want. The dead kings. Have you seen any of them?"

"No. But I know they're out there. Thinking." He brooded at the strip of woods along the pastures. "What in Hel's name would they want with my cattle? The teeth of these kings are scattered all over my fields. King Farr's skull has been grinning above the hearth in the great hall for centuries; what is he going to eat with?"

Her eyes slid from the unstirred woods back to his face. "His skull?" An idea flickered in the back of her mind. Hallard nodded tiredly.

"Supposedly. Some dauntless rebel stole his head from Oen, the tale goes, after Oen crowned it and stuck it on a spearhead in his kitchen-midden. Years later it found its way back here, with the crown cut and melded again to fit bare bone. Mag Blackdawn, whose father had died in that war, was still angry enough to nail it like a battle emblem, crown and all, above his hearthfire. After so many centuries the gold has worn into the bone; you can't keep one without the other. That's why I don't understand," he added at a tangent. "Why they're troubling my lands; they're my ancestors."

"There were lords of An killed here, too," she suggested. "Maybe they were the ones in your wheat fields. Hallard, I want that skull."

"You what?"

"Farr's skull. I want it."

He stared at her. She saw, gazing back at him, the faint struggle in him as he tried to shift her back to her place in his known world. "What for?"

"Just give it to me."

"In Hel's name, what for?" he shouted, then stopped and closed his eyes again. "I'm sorry. You're starting to sound like your father; he has a gift for making me shout. Now. Let's both try to be rational—"

"I was never less interested in being rational in my life. I want that skull. I want you to go into your great hall and take it off your wall without damaging it and wrap it in velvet and give it to me at your—"

"Velvet!" he exploded. "Are you mad?"

She thought about it for a split second and shouted back at him. "Maybe! But not so I would care! Yes, velvet! Would you want to look at your own skull on a piece of sacking?"

His horse jerked, as though he had pulled it involuntarily back from her. His lips parted; she heard his quick breathing as he struggled for words. Then he reached out slowly, put his hand on her forearm. "Raederle." He spoke her name like a reminder to them both. "What are you going to do with it?"

She swallowed, her own mouth going dry as she contemplated her intentions. "Hallard, the Star-Bearer is crossing your land—"

His voice rose again incredulously. "Now?"

She nodded. "And behind him—behind me, fol-

lowing him, is something . . . maybe the Founder of
Lungold. I can't protect Morgon from him, but
maybe I can keep the dead of An from betraying
his presence—"

"With a skull?"

"Will you keep your voice down!"

He rubbed his face with his hands. "Madir's
bones. The Star-Bearer can take care of himself."

"Even he might be a little pressed by the Founder
and the unbound forces of An all at once." Her voice
steadied. "He is going to Anuin; I want to see that he
gets there. If—"

"No."

"If you don't—"

"No." His head was shaking slowly back and
forth. "No."

"Hallard." She held his eyes. "If you don't give
me that skull now, I will lay a curse on your threshold that no friend will ever cross it, on the high gates
and posterns and stable doors that they will never
close again, on the torches in your house that they
will never burn, on your hearth stones that no one
standing under Farr's hollow eyes will ever feel
warm. This I swear by my name. If you don't give
me that skull I will rouse the dead of An, myself, on
your land in the name of the King of An and ride
with them into war on your fields against the ancient
Kings of Hel. This I swear by my name. If you
don't—"

"All right!"

His cry echoed, furious and desperate, across his
lands. His face was patched white under his tan; he
stared at her, breathing hard, while blackbirds
startled up from the trees behind them and his men
shifted their mounts uneasily in the distance. "All
right," he whispered. "Why not? The whole of An is
in chaos, why shouldn't you ride around with a dead
king's skull in your hands? But, woman, I hope you

know what you're doing. Because if you are harmed, you will lay a curse of grief and guilt across my threshold, and until I die no fire in my hearth will ever be great enough to warm me." He wheeled his horse without waiting for her to answer; she followed him down through his fields, across the river to his gates, feeling the frightened blood pounding in her ears like footsteps.

She waited, still mounted, while he went inside. She could see through the open gates the empty yard. Not even the forge fire was lit; there were no stray animals, no children shouting in the corners, only the incessant, invisible baying of hounds. Hallard reappeared shortly, a round object gathered in the folds of a length of rich, red velvet. He handed it to her wordlessly; she opened the velvet, caught a glimpse of white bone with gold melting into it and said, "There's one more thing I want."

"What if it's not his head?" He watched her. "Legends are spun around so many lies—"

"It had better be," she whispered. "I need a necklace of glass beads. Can you find one for me?"

"Glass beads." He covered his eyes with his fingers and groaned like the hounds. Then he flung up his hands and turned again. He was gone longer this time; the expression on his face when he came back was, if possible, more harassed. He dangled a small, sparkling circle of round, clear beads in front of her; a simple necklace that a trader might have given away to a young girl or a hard-worked farmer's wife. "They'll look fine rattling among Farr's bones." Then, as she reached down to take it, he grasped her wrist again. "Please," he whispered. "I gave you the skull. Now come into my house, out of danger. I can't let you ride through Hel. It's quiet now, but when night falls, there's not a man who will stir beyond his barred doors; you'll be alone out there in the darkness with the name you bear and all the twisted hatred of the old lords of Hel. All the small powers you have inherited will not be enough to help you. Please—"

She pulled loose of him, backed her horse. "Then I'll have to test the powers of another heritage. If I don't come back, it will not matter."

"Raederle!"

She felt the sound of her own name spin out over his lands, echo in the deep woods and places of secret gatherings. She rode swiftly away from his house before he could follow her. She went downriver to his southern fields, where the young wheat lay whipped and churned and the ancient graves of Hallard's ancestors, once smooth green swellings whose doors had sunk waist-deep in the earth, were smashed like eggs. She reined in front of them. Through the dark crumbled soil and the broken foundation stones she could see the pale glint of rich arms no living man dared touch. She lifted her head. The woods were motionless; the summer sky stretched endlessly over An, cloudless and peaceful, except toward the west where the blue gathered to a dark, intense line above the oak. She turned her horse again, looked out over the empty, whispering fields. She said softly into the wind, "Farr, I have your head. If you want it, to lie with your bones under the earth of Hel, then come and get it."

She spent the rest of the afternoon gathering wood on the edge of the trees above the barrows. As the sun went down she lit a fire and unwrapped the skull from its velvet coverings. It was discolored with age and soot; the gold banding its wide brow was riveted to the bone. The teeth, she noted, were intact in the tightly clenched jaws; the deep eyepits and wide, jutting cheekbone gave her a hint of the king whose head had stared, furious and unsubmissive, over Oen's midden. The firelight rippled the shadows in the eye sockets, and her mouth dried.

She spread the bright cloth, laid the skull on top of it. Then she drew the necklace of glass beads out of her pocket, bound an image in her mind to them with her name. She dropped them into the fire. All around her, enclosing the skull, the firewood and her uneasy mount, rose a luminous circle of huge, fiery moons.

At moonrise, she heard the cattle in Hallard's barn begin to bawl. Dogs in the small farms beyond the trees set up a constant chorus of shrill, startled barking. Something that was not the wind sighed through the oak, and Raederle's shoulders hunched as it passed over her head. Her horse, lying beside her, scrambled to its feet, trembling. She tried to speak to it soothingly, but the words stuck in her throat. There was a great crashing in the distant trees; animals lying quiet until then, began to stir and flee before it. A stag running blind, reared and belled as it came suddenly upon the strange, fiery circle, wrenched itself around and shot towards the open fields. Small deer, foxes, weasels roused in the night, bounded silently, desperately past her, pursued by the rending of branches and underbrush, and a weird, unearthly bellow that shattered again and again through the trees. Raederle, shuddering, her hands icy, her thoughts scattering like blown chaff, added branch after branch to the fire until the beads swam red with flame. She stopped herself from burning all the wood at once by sheer will, and stood, her hands over her mouth to keep her heart from leaping free, waiting for the nightmare to emerge from the dark.

It came in the shape of the great White Bull of Aum. The enormous animal, whom Cyn Croeg loved as Raith of Hel loved his pig herds, loomed out of the night towards her flames, pricked and driven by riders whose mounts, yellow, rust, black, were lean, rangey, evil-eyed. Their heads snaking sideways, they nipped at the bull as they ran. The bull, flecked with blood and sweat, his flat, burly face maddened and terrified, swung past Raederle's circle so closely she could see his rimmed eyes and smell the musk of his fear. The riders swarmed about him as he turned, ignoring her, except the last who, turning a grinning face her direction, showed her the seam of the scar across his face that ended in a white, withered eye.

All sounds around her seemed to dwindle to one point inside her head; she wondered, dimly, if she was going to faint. The groan of the bull in the distance made her open her eyes again. She saw it, gigantic and ash-colored under the moonlight, blundering with its horns lowered across Hallard's fields. The riders, their arms flickering a bluish-silver like lightning, seemed mercilessly intent upon driving it into Hallard's closed gates. There they would leave it, she knew in a sudden, terrible flash of insight, like a gift at Hallard's doorway, a dead weight of bull for him to explain somehow to the Lord of Aum. She wondered, in that split second, how Raith's pigs were faring. Then her horse screamed behind her and she whirled, gasping, to face the wraith of King Farr of Hel.

He was, as she imagined him, a big, powerful man with a wide slab of a face hard as a slammed gate. His beard and long hair were copper; he wore rings of hard metal at every knuckle, and his sword, rising above one of the glass moons, was broad at the base as the length of his hand. He wasted no time with words; the sword, cutting down into the thin air of illusion, nearly wrenched him off his horse. He straightened, tried to ride his horse through it, but the animal balked with a squeal of pain and cast a furious eye at him. He reined it back to try to leap; Raederle, reaching for the skull, held it above the flames.

"I'll drop it," she warned breathlessly. "And then I will take it, black with ash, to Anuin and throw it back in the midden."

"You will not live," he said. The voice was in her mind; she saw then the ragged, scarlet weal at his throat. He cursed her in his hoarse, hollow voice, thoroughly and methodically, from head to foot, in language she had never heard any man use.

Her face was burning when he finished; she dangled the skull by one finger in an eye socket over the flames and said tersely, "Do you want this or not? Shall I use it for kindling?"

"You'll burn up your wood by dawn," the implacable voice said. "I'll take it then."

"You'll never take it." Her own voice, colored with anger, sounded with a dead certainty that she almost felt. "Believe that. Your bones lie rotting in the fields of a man whose allegiance is sworn to An, and only you remember what shinbones and snapped neckbone belong to you. If you had this crown, it might give you the dignity of remembrance, but you'll never take it from me. If I choose, I'll give it to you. For a price."

"I bargain with no man. I submit to no man. Least of all to a woman spawned out of the Kings of An."

"I am spawned out of worse than that. I will give you your skull for one price only. If you refuse me once, I will destroy it. I want an escort of Kings through Hel and into Anuin for one man—"

"Anuin!" The word reverberated painfully in her own skull and she winced. "I will never—"

"I will ask only once. The man is a stranger to An, a shape-changer. He is moving in fear of his life through An, and I want him hidden and protected. Following him is the greatest wizard of the realm; he'll try to stop you, but you will not submit. If the man is harmed on the way to Anuin by this wizard, your crowned skull is forfeit." She paused, added temperately, "Whatever else you do on your journey through An will be your own business, as long as he is protected. I'll give you the skull in the house of the Kings of An."

He was silent. She realized suddenly that the night had grown very quiet; even Haggard Blackdawn's hounds were still. She wondered if they were all dead. Then she wondered, almost idly, what Duac would say when he found the wraiths of the Kings of Hel in his house. Farr's voice seeped into her thoughts.

"And after?"

"After?"

"After we reach Anuin? What demands, what restrictions will you place on us in your own house?"

She drew breath, and found no more courage left in her for demands. "If the man is safe, none. If you have kept him safe. But I want an escort of Kings of Hel only, not a gathering of the army of the dead."

There was another long silence. She dragged a branch onto the fire, saw the flick of calculation in his eyes. Then he said unexpectedly, "Who is this man?"

"If you don't know his name, no one can take it from you. You know the shapes of Hel: trees, animals, the earth; you are of them, rooted with them. Find the stranger whose outward shape is of An, whose core is of nothing of An."

"If he is nothing of An, then what is he to you?"

"What do you think?" she asked wearily. "When I'm sitting here alone for his sake in the roused night of Hel bargaining with a dead king over his skull?"

"You're a fool."

"Maybe. But you're bargaining, too."

"I do not bargain. An deprived me of my crown, and An will give it back to me. One way or another. I'll give you my answer at dawn. If your fire goes out before then, beware. I will show you no more mercy than Oen of An showed to me."

He settled himself to wait, his face, baleful and unblinking, rising out of the darkness above the fiery beads. She wanted to scream at him suddenly that she had nothing to do with his feuds or his death, that he had been dead for centuries and his vengeance was a matter insignificant in the turmoil of events beyond An. But his brain was alive only in the past, and the long centuries must have seemed to him the passing of a single night over Hel. She sat down in front of the fire, her mouth papery. She wondered if, when dawn came, he intended to kill her or to barter with Duac over her as she had bartered over his skull. Hallard Blackdawn's house, with all its windows lit at that hour, across two fields and the river, seemed as far away as a dream. As she gazed at it helplessly, the din began again in the fields, a new sound this time: the chilling clash of weapons in a night battle in Hallard's cow pasture. The hounds bayed the danger hoarsely, imperatively, like battle horns. The eyes of the King met hers over the illusion of fire, relentless, assured. She looked down from him to the fire and saw the small, blazing circle, the core of the illusion, the glass beads cracking slowly in the tempering of the fire.

The cries faded to a corner of her mind. She heard the snap of wood, the sibilant language of the flames. She opened her hand, touched an angle of flame and watched the reflection of it in her mind. It groped for her shape as she held it in her mind and her hand; she kept her own thoughts mute, tapped a silence deeply within her mind which it slowly moved and gathered. She let it gather for a long time, sitting motionless as the ancient trees around her, her hand uplifted, open to the flame that traced constantly the twelve-sided figure on her palm. Then a shadow flowed over her mind, quenching the fire in it: another mind spanning the night, drawing into its vortex a comprehension of the living and dead of An. It passed like great, dark wings blocking the moon and brought her back, shivering and defenseless, into the night. She closed her hand quickly over the small flame and looked up to see the first hint of expression in Farr's eyes.

"What was that?" His voice rasped jarringly in her head.

She felt his mind unexpectedly and knew that she was beginning to startle him, too. She said, "That is what you will protect the Star—the stranger from."

"That?"

"That." She added after a moment, "He'll blot out your wraith like a candle if he realizes what you are doing and nothing will be left of you but your bones and a memory. Do you want your skull so badly now?"

"I want it," he said grimly. "Either here or at Anuin, Witch. Take your choice."

"I'm not a witch."

"What are you, then, with your eyes full of fire?"

She thought about it. Then she said simply, "I am nameless," while something too bitter for sorrow touched the back of her mouth. She turned again to the fire, added more wood to it, followed the wild flight of each spark to its vanishing point. She cupped the fire again, this time in both hands, and began slowly to shape it.

She was interrupted many times during the endless night: by the run of Hallard Blackdawn's stolen cattle, bawling in terror across his wheat fields; by the gathering of armed men around Farr as he waited, and his bellow of fury in her mind when they laughed at him; by the flurry of sword play that followed. She lifted her head once and saw only his bare bones on his horse, blurred with fire; another time, she saw his head like a helm in the crook of his arm, his expression changeless while her eyes groped for shape above the stump of his neck. Near dawn, when the moon set, she had forgotten him, forgotten everything. She had drawn the flames into a hundred varied shapes, flowers that opened then melted away, fiery birds that took wing from her hand. She had forgotten even her own shape; her hands, weaving in and out of the fire, seemed one more shape of it. Something undefined, unexpected, was happening in her mind. Glimpses of power, knowledge, elusive as the fire, passed before her mind's eye, as though she had wakened within her memories of her heritage. Faces, shadows stretching beyond her knowledge formed and vanished under her probing; strange plants, sea languages whispered just beyond her hearing. A void in the depth of the sea, or at the heart of the world, cut a hollow through her mind; she gazed into it fearlessly, curiously, too lost within her work to wonder whose black thought it was. She kindled a distant star of fire even in that barren waste. She felt then, as it stirred, that it was no void, but a tangle of memory and power on the verge of definition.

That knowledge sent her groping urgently for the simpler chaos of An. She came to rest like a weary traveller within herself. The dawn mists lay over Hallard's fields; the ash-colored morning hung amid the trees without a sound to welcome it. All that remained of her night fire was the charred stubble of branches. She stirred stiffly, sleepily, then saw the hand out of the corner of her eye, reaching for the skull.

She set it blazing with an illusion of fire from her mind; Farr flinched back. She picked up the skull and rose, stood facing him. He whispered, "You are made of fire . . ."

She felt it in her fingers, running beneath the skin, in the roots of her hair. She said, her voice cracking

with tiredness, "Have you made up your mind?
You'll never find Oen here; his bones lie in the
Field of Kings outside of Anuin. If you can survive
the journey, you can take your revenge there."

"Do you betray your own family?"

"Will you give me an answer?" she cried, stung;
and he was silent, struggling. She felt his yielding
before he spoke, and she whispered, "Swear by your
name. Swear by the crown of the Kings of Hel. That
neither you nor anyone else will touch me or this
skull until you have crossed the threshold at Anuin."

"I swear it."

"That you will gather the kings as you journey
across Hel, to find and protect the shape of the stranger travelling to Anuin, against all living, against all
dead."

"I swear it."

"That you will tell no one but the Kings of Hel
what you are sworn to do."

"I swear it. By my name, in the name of the
Kings of Hel and by this crown."

He looked, dismounted in the dawn light with the
taste of submission in his mouth, almost alive. She
drew a soundless breath and loosed it. "All right. I
swear in my father's name and in the name of the
man you will escort, that when I see him in the
King's house at Anuin, I will give you your skull and
ask nothing further from you. All binding between
us will end. The only other thing I ask is that you let
me know when you find him."

He gave a brief nod. His eyes met the black, hollow, mocking gaze of the skull. Then he turned and
mounted. He looked down at her a moment before
he left, and she saw the disbelief in his eyes. Then
he rode away, noiseless as a drift of leaves beneath
the trees.

She met, as she herself rode out of the woods,
Hallard Blackdawn and his men venturing out to

count the dead cattle in the lower fields. He stared at her; his voice, when he found it finally, was strengthless.

"Oen's right hand. Is it you or a ghost?"

"I don't know. Is Cyn Croeg's bull dead?"

"They ran the life out of it . . . Come to the house." His eyes, the shock wearing away from them, held a strange expression: half-solicitous, half-awed. His hand rose hesitantly, touched her. "Come in. You look—you look—"

"I know. But I can't. I'm going to Anuin."

"Now? Wait, I'll give you an escort."

"I have one." She watched his eyes fall to the skull riding the pommel of her saddle; he swallowed.

"Did he come for it?"

She smiled slightly. "He came. We did some bargaining—"

"Oen's right—" He shuddered unashamedly. "No one ever bargained with Farr. For what? The safety of Anuin?"

She drew breath. "Well, no. Not exactly." She took the necklace out of her pocket and gave it to him. "Thank you. I couldn't have survived without it."

Glancing back once, as she reached down to open a field gate, she saw him standing motionlessly beside a dead bullock, still staring at the worthless handful of cracked, fired beads.

She crossed the length of Hel as far as Raith's lands with a growing, invisible escort of Kings. She felt them around her, groped for their minds until they gave her their names: Acor, third King of Hel, who had brought through force and persuasion the last of the bickering lords under his control; Ohroe the Cursed, who had seen seven of his nine sons fall one after another in seven consecutive battles between Hel and An; Nemir of the Pigs, who had spoken the language of both men and pigs, who had bred the boar Hegdis-Noon and had as his pigherder the witch Madir; Evern the Falconer, who trained hawks for battle against men; and others, all Kings, as Farr had sworn, who joined him, the last of the Kings, in his journey to the stronghold of the Kings of An. She rarely saw them; she felt them range before and behind her, their minds joining in a network of thought, legend, plots, remembrances of Hel during their lives, after their deaths. They were still bound to the earth of An, more than even they realized; their minds slid easily in and out of different shapes that their bones had become entwined with: roots, leaves, insects, the small bodies of animals. It was through this deep, wordless knowledge of An, Raederle knew, that they recognized the Star-Bearer, the man whose shape would hold none of the essence of An.

They had found him swiftly. Farr broke his silence to tell her that; she did not ask what shape he had taken. The Kings surrounded him loosely as he moved: the hart, perhaps, that bounded in terror across a moonlit field at their presence; the bird startled into flight; the fieldmouse scuttling through broken shafts of hay. She guessed that he dared not keep one shape long, but she was surprised that the Kings never once lost track of him. They were a decoy to the powerful mind she glimpsed occasionally as it groped over the land. No man of An, and certainly no stranger, could have passed among them unnoticed; the wizard, she guessed, must search every man they did meet. She was surprised also that he did not threaten her as she rode alone through the troubled land; perhaps he thought, seeing the skull on her saddle, watching her sleep at nights in the woods impervious to the tumult around her, that she was mad.

She avoided people, so she had no news of the extent of the trouble, but she saw, again and again, empty fields at midday, barns and stables locked and guarded, lords travelling with armed retinues towards Anuin. Their tempers, she knew, must be worn thin by the constant harassment; they would, in time, turn their houses into small, armed fortresses, draw into themselves and soon trust no man, living or dead. The mistrust and the anger against the absent King of An would fester into open war, a great battleground of living and dead, that not even Mathom would be able to control. And she, bringing the Kings of Hel into Anuin, might precipitate it.

She thought much about that, lying sleepless at night with the skull beside her. She tried to prepare for it, exploring her powers, but she had little experience to guide her. She was dimly aware of what she might be able to do, of powers intangible as shadows in her mind, powers she could not yet quite grasp and control. She would do what she could at Anuin; Morgon, if he could risk it, would help. Perhaps Mathom would return; perhaps the Kings would retreat from Anuin without an army behind them. Perhaps she could find something else to barter with. She hoped Duac, in some small measure, would understand. But she doubted it.

She reached Anuin nine days after she had left Hallard's land. The Kings had begun to appear before they entered the gates, riding in a grim, amazing escort about the man they guarded. The streets of the city seemed fairly untroubled; there were quite a few people out staring, uneasy and astonished, at the group of riders with their nervous, wicked mounts, their crowned heads, armbands and brooches of gold, their arms and rich clothes spanning nearly the entire history of the land. Among them, cloaked and hooded in the warm day, rode the man they had been guarding. He seemed resigned to his unearthly escort; he rode without a glance at it, slowly and steadily through the streets of Anuin, up the gentle slope to the house of the King. The gates were open; they rode unchallenged into the yard. They dismounted, to the confusion of the grooms, who had no intention, even under the weight of Farr's hot gaze, of taking their horses. Raederle, riding alone into the gates behind them, saw them follow the cloaked figure up the steps to the hall. The expression in the grooms' faces as they hesitated around her made her realize that they thought she, too, might be a wraith. Then one came forward uncertainly to hold her reins and stirrup as she dismounted. She took the skull from the pommel, carried it with her into the hall.

She found Duac alone in the hall, staring, speechless, at the collection of Kings. His mouth was open; as she entered, his eyes flicked to her and she heard it click closed. The blood ran out of his face, leaving it the color of Farr's skull. She wondered, as she went towards the hooded man, why he did not turn and speak to her. He turned then, as though he had felt her thoughts, and she found her own mouth dropped open. The man the Kings had followed and guarded through Hel had not been Morgon but Deth.

10

SHE STOPPED SHORT, STARING AT HIM IN UTTER disbelief. The skin was strained taut, blanched against the bones of his face; he looked, haunted for nine days by the wraiths of Hel, as though he had not slept much. She breathed, "You." She looked at Farr, who was running a calculating eye over the beams and corners of the house. Duac, who had begun to move, finally, was coming towards her carefully through the assortment of Kings. They were standing silently, expectantly, their strange shields scrolled with nameless animals deflecting flat, burning fields of light from the windows. Her heart began to hammer suddenly. She found her voice again, and Farr's head turned sharply as she spoke, "What are you doing here? I left you in the backlands going to Lungold."

The familiar, even voice sounded frayed, almost tight. "I had no desire to meet the Morgol or her guards in the backlands. I sailed down the Cwill to Hlurle, and found passage on a ship to Caithnard. There are not many places in the realm left open to me."

"So you came here?"

"It is one last place."

"Here." She drew breath and shouted at him in sudden, furious despair, halting Duac mid-pace, "You came here, and because of you I have let all the Kings of Hel into this house!" She heard the hollow rasp of Farr's question in her brain, and she turned on him. "You brought the wrong man! He isn't even a shape-changer!"

"We found him in that shape, and he chose to keep it," Farr answered, in his surprise momentarily defensive. "He was the only stranger moving secretly through Hel."

"He couldn't have been! What kind of a poor bargain was it that you kept? You would have had to search all the back streets and docksides of the realm to find a man I wanted less to see."

"I kept the vows I swore." She could tell by Duac's expression that the harsh, unearthly voice was rebounding also in his mind. "The skull is mine. The binding is finished."

"No." She backed a step from him, her fingers locked tightly around the lidless gaze and grin of the skull. "You left the man you swore to guard somewhere in Hel, to be harried by the dead, to be discovered by—"

"There was no one else!" She saw even Deth wince slightly at his exasperated shout. He stepped towards her, his eyes dark smoldering. "Woman, you are bound by your name to your own vow, to the bargain that brought me across this threshold where Oen carried that skull and my last curse with it and throned me king of his midden. If you don't give me that skull, I swear by—"

"You will swear nothing." She gathered light from the shields, kindled it in her mind, and laid it like a yellow bar in front of him. "And you will not touch me."

"Can you control us all, Witch?" he asked grimly. "Try."

"Wait," Duac said abruptly. He held a hand, palm outward, in the air, as Farr's baleful gaze swung at him. "Wait." The authority of desperation in his voice held Farr momentarily at bay. Duac stepped cautiously past the light on the floor, reached Raederle and put his hands on her shoulders. She saw, looking up at him, Ylon's face briefly, the pale, angled brows, the eyes uneasy with color. Her shoulders flinched slightly at the sudden human touch, when she had spoken to nothing human for nine days, and she saw the anguish break into his eyes. He whispered, "What have you done to yourself? And to this house?"

She wanted, gazing back at him, to spread the whole tangled tale out for him, to make him understand why her hair hung lank and dirty to her waist, why she was arguing with a dead king over his skull and could seemingly shape pure air into flame. But in the face of Farr's anger she dared yield nothing. She said stiffly, "We made a bargain, Farr and I—"

"Farr." His lips shaped the word almost without sound, and she nodded, swallowing drily.

"I made Hallard Blackdawn give me his skull. I sat up all night during the rousing of Hel, circled by fire, working with fire, and by dawn I had the power to bargain. The Star-Bearer was coming through Hel to Anuin; Farr swore to gather Kings to protect him in exchange for the skull. He swore by his own name and the names of the Kings of Hel. But he didn't keep his part of the bargain. He didn't even try to find a shape-changer; he simply guarded the first stranger who he found travelling across Hel—"

"The stranger made no objection." The cold

voice of Evern the Falconer cut across her words.
"He was being hunted. He used our protection."

"Of course he was hunted! He—" Then the realization slapped at her, of the true extent of the
danger she had brought into her house. She whispered, her fingers icy against the bone in her hands,
"Duac—" But his eyes had flicked away from her
face to the harpist.

"Why did you come here? The Star-Bearer has
not reached Anuin yet, but you must have known
the traders would bring his tale."

"I thought your father might have returned."

"What," Duac inquired more in wonder than
anger, "in Hel's name would you expect my father
to say to you?"

"Very little." He stood with a haunting, familiar
quiescence, but there was a preoccupation in his
face, as though he were listening for something beyond their hearing. Raederle touched Duac's arm.

"Duac." Her voice shook. "Duac. I am bringing
more than the Kings of Hel into Anuin."

He closed his eyes, breathed something. "What
now? You vanished two months ago from Caithnard, took our father's ship and left Rood to ride
home alone without the faintest idea of where you
were. Now you appear out of nowhere, with as
much warning, accompanied by the Kings of Hel,
an outlawed harpist and a crowned skull. The walls
of this house could cave in on my head next and I
doubt if I'd be surprised." He paused a moment;
his hold tightened. "Are you all right?"

She shook her head, still whispering. "No. Oh,
no. Duac, I was trying to guard Morgon against
Ghisteslwchlohm."

"Ghisteslwchlohm?"

"He is—he followed Deth through Hel."

The expression died on his face. His eyes went
beyond her to Deth, and then he lifted his hands

carefully off her shoulders as though he were lifting stones. "All right." There was no hope in his voice. "Maybe we can—"

The harpist's voice, sprung taut, interrupted him. "The Founder is nowhere in An."

"I felt him!" Raederle cried. "He was behind you at the gates of Anuin. I felt his mind searching all the corners of Hel; he would break through my mind like a black wind, and I could feel his hatred, his rage—"

"That is not the Founder."

"Then who—" She stopped. The men, living and dead, seemed motionless as figures on a chessboard around her. She shook her head slowly, mute again, while the bone strained under her grip.

The harpist said with unexpected intensity, "I would never have chosen this place. But you didn't give me a choice."

"Morgon?" she whispered. She remembered then his quick, silent departure from Caithnard, the lawless mind that had found her, yet never threatened her. "I brought you here so he could kill you?" His face, hopeless, exhausted, gave her his answer. Something between a shout and a sob of grief and confusion welled through her. She stared at Deth, breathing tightly, feeling the hot swell of tears behind her eyes. "There are things not worth killing. Curse us all for this: you for making him what he has become; him for not seeing what he has become; and me for bringing you nearly face-to-face. You will destroy him even with your death. There's the door, open. Find a ship out of Anuin—"

"To where?"

"Anywhere! To the bottom of the sea, if nowhere else. Go harp with Ylon's bones, I don't care. Just go, so far he'll forget your name and your memory. Go—"

"It's too late." His voice was almost gentle. "You have brought me into your house."

She heard a step behind her and whirled. But it was Rood, flushed and dishevelled from riding, coming precipitously into the hall. He cast a crow-colored eye at the assembly of wraiths pulled out of their graves by a dream of revenge, armed as no King of An had armed himself for centuries. He stopped short; Raederle saw, even as his face whitened, the gleam of recognition in his eyes. Then Ohroe the Cursed, standing near him, whose face was seamed red from temple to jaw with his death wound, gripped the neck of Rood's tunic and wrenched him backward. His arm, heavy with chain mail, locked tightly around Rood's throat; a knife flashed in his other hand; the point of it pricked Rood's own temple. He said succinctly, "Now. Let us bargain again." Raederle's terrified, furious rill of thought blazed white-hot across the knife blade and leaped into Ohroe's eyes. He gasped, dropping the knife. Rood's elbow slamming into the mailed ribs seemed to have no effect, but the arm around his throat loosened as Ohroe lifted his hand to his head. Rood slipped free, pausing as he crossed the hall only to pull off the wall an ancient blade that had hung there since Hagis's death. He joined Duac who said tersely, "Will you put that sword down? The last thing I want is a pitched battle in this house."

The Kings seemed to be shifting together without sound. Among them, the harpist, his head lowered slightly as though his attention were focussed on nothing of the movement around him, was conspicuous in his stillness, and Rood made a sound in his throat. He took a firmer grip on the sword hilt and said, "Tell them that. At least when we're wraiths ourselves, we can fight on our own terms. Who brought them here? Deth?"

"Raederle."

Rood's head turned sharply. He saw Raederle, then, standing a little behind Duac. His eyes went from her worn face to the skull in her hands, and the sword tip struck the floor with a clink. She saw a shudder rack through him.

"Raederle? I saw you and I didn't even recognize you . . ." He flung the sword on the stones and went to her. He reached out to her as Duac had, but his hands dropped before he touched her. He gazed at her, and she saw that, deep in him. something dormant. unfamiliar to him. was struggling with the sense of her power. He whispered, "What happened to you? What happens to people who try to make that journey to Erlenstar Mountain?"

She swallowed, lifted one hand away from the skull to touch him. "Rood—"

"Where did you get such power? It's like nothing you ever had before."

"I always had it—"

"From what? I look at you now, and I don't even know who you are!"

"You know me," she whispered, her throat burning. "I am of An . . ."

"Rood," Duac said. His voice held an odd, flat tone of apprehension that pulled Rood's eyes from Raederle's face. Duac was staring at the doorway; he groped behind him for Rood. "Rood. That. Who is that? Tell me it's not who I think it is—"

Rood swung around. Crossing the threshold, soundless, shadowless, on a great black mount whose eyes were the color of the eyes of Farr's skull, rode a man with a single blood-red jewel on the circle of gold on his head. He was dark, sinewy, powerful; the hilts of his knife and sword were of braided gold; the rich coat over his mail was embroidered with the ancient emblem of An:

an oak holding a bolt of black lightning in its green boughs. He left a following on the threshold that must have come out of the fields and orchards around Anuin. Beyond them, through the open doors, Raederle could see Duac's own guards and unarmed servants struggling to get through. They might as well have struggled against a stone wall. The effect of the crowned man on the wraiths in the hall was immediate: every sword in the room was drawn. Farr moved forward, his flat, expressionless face livid above the cut on his neck, the huge blade raised in his hand. The dead King's eyes, ignoring Farr, moving slowly over the gathering, touched Duac. The black horse stopped.

"Oen."

Rood's voice drew the King's attention to him briefly, then his gaze returned to Duac. His head bent slightly, he said, his voice temperless yet inflexible, "Peace be on the living in this house, and may no dishonor come into it. To those with honor." He paused, his eyes still on Duac's face as he recognized the ageless instinct in him for land-law, together with something else. He gave a short laugh that held little amusement. "You have a face out of the sea. But your own father is more fortunate. You bear little more of my land-heir than his memory . . ."

Duac, looking harrowed, found his voice finally. "Peace—" The word shook, and he swallowed. "Will you bring peace with you into this house and leave it behind when you go."

"I cannot. I have sworn a vow. Beyond death." Duac's eyes closed, his lips moving in a succinct, inaudible curse. Oen's face turned finally to Farr; their eyes met across the room for the first time outside of their dreams in six centuries. "I swore that as long as the Kings ruled Anuin, Farr of Hel would rule the king's midden."

"And I have sworn," Farr rasped, "that I would not close my eyes in my grave until those ruling Anuin were lying in theirs."

Oen's brow flicked upward. "You lost your head once before. I heard that a woman of Anuin carried your skull out of Hel, back to this house and to her shame opened the doors of this house to the dead of Hel. I have come to cleanse it of the smell of the midden." He glanced at Raederle. "Give me the skull."

She stood dumbfounded at the contempt in his voice, in his eyes, the dark, calculating eyes that had watched a tower with iron bars at its windows being built for his land-heir beside the sea. "You," she whispered, "bringing empty words into this house, what did you ever know of peace? You small-minded man, content in your battles, you left a riddle behind you in Anuin when you died that was far more than just a sea-colored face. You want to fight with Farr over this skull like dogs over a bone. You think I betrayed my house: what do you know of betrayal? You have roused yourself for revenge: what do you know of revenge? You think you saw the last of Ylon's strange powers when you walled him in his tower so efficiently with such little understanding, such little compassion. You should have known that you cannot bind a sorrow or an anger. You have waited six centuries for a battle with Farr. Well, before you raise your sword in this hall, you will have to fight me."

She stripped light from the shields, from the armbands and jewelled crowns, from the flagstones, blazed a circle on the stones around Oen. She looked for a single source of fire in the room, but there was not even a candle lit. So she contented herself with drawing it out of her memory, the shapeless, flickering element she had mastered under Farr's ominous gaze. She laid the illusion of it around the illusions of the dead. She opened her hand and showed them how she could shape with it, drawing it high into the air, sending it spattering like waves breaking against her will. She circled them with it, as she had been forced by them to circle herself, watched them close together away from it. She burnished the shields with flame, saw them drop, soundless as flowers, to the floor. She ringed the crowns with it, watched the Kings send them spinning, wheels of flaming metal, into the air. She heard the voices, faraway, indistinct, birds' voices, the fragmented voice of the sea. Then she heard the sea itself.

The sound of it wove in and out of her shaping. She recognized the slow break and drag of it; the hollow wind moaning through broken iron bars. The harping was ended; the tower was empty. She drew her attention back to Oen; half-blind with the thought of fire, she saw him only as a shadow, hunched a little on his horse. And a fury that did not belong to her but to his roused land-heir began gathering in her like one enormous wave that might have torn the tower out of the rocks by its roots and flung it into the sea.

The fury gave her dark insight into odd powers. It whispered to her how to crack a solid flagstone in two, how to turn the thin, black rift into a yawning illusion of emptiness that would drain the wraith of Oen, nameless, memoryless, into it. It showed her how to bind the windows and doors of her own house, lock the living and dead in it; how to create the illusion of one door in it opening constantly to an illusion of freedom. It showed her how to separate the hopeless essence of sorrow she felt from the sea, the wind, the memory of the harping, to work it into the stones and shadows of the house so that no one in it would ever laugh. She felt her own sorrow and anger stirred, as she had kindled the light, mixed with an older agony and rage against Oen until she could barely tell them apart; she could barely remember that Oen was to her simply a memory of An, and not the living, terrible, merciless figure of Ylon's memory.

She felt herself lost, drowning in the force of another's hatred. She struggled against it, blind, terrified, not knowing how to break free of the determined impulse to destruction aimed against Oen. Her terror gave way to a helpless anger; she was bound, as Oen had bound Ylon, by hatred, by compassionlessness, and by misunderstanding. She realized, before she destroyed Oen, before she loosed something alien to the very land-law of An into the house of its kings, that she had to force the wraith of Ylon, roused in her, to see clearly for the first time, the heritage they both shared, and the King who had been simply a man bound to its patterns.

One by one, with impossible effort, she drew the faces of the Kings out of the firelight. She wrested out of the dark void of rage and sorrow, names for them, histories, spoke their names as, weaponless, crownless, mute, they faced her again across the hall: Acor, Ohroe, cursed with sorrow for his sons, Nemir who spoke pig-language, Farr who had done her bidding for the sake of a six-hundred-year-old skull, Evern who had died with his falcons, defending his home. The fire dwindled away around them, became sunlight on the flagstones. She saw the High One's harpist again among the Kings. She saw Oen. He was no longer on his horse, but standing beside it. His face was bowed against its back. She saw then the black, jagged break from end to end in the flagstone at his feet.

She said his name. The naming seemed to shift him to perspective: the frightened wraith of a dead man who had once been, centuries ago, a King of An. The hatred in her roused only weakly against him, against the power of her seeing. It roused again, then drained away like a spent wave. It left her free, gazing at the broken stone, wondering what name she would bear for the rest of her life in that hall.

She found herself trembling so badly she could hardly stand. Rood, beside her, lifted his hand to hold her, but he seemed to have no strength either; he could not touch her. She saw Duac staring at the flagstone. He turned his head slowly, looked at her. A sob burned in her throat, for he had no name for her either. Her power had left her placeless, had left her nothing. Her eyes fell away from him to a strip of darkness at her feet between them. She realized slowly that the darkness was a shadow that stretched across the floor in a hall full of shadowless dead.

She turned. The Star-Bearer stood at the threshold. He was alone; Oen's following had vanished. He was watching her; she knew from the expression in his eyes, how much he had seen. As she gazed at him helplessly, he said softly, "Raederle." It was no warning, no judgment, simply her name, and she could have wept at the recognition in it.

He moved, finally, across the threshold. Plainly clothed, seemingly unarmed, he walked almost unobtrusively among the silent Kings, and yet one by one he drew their attention to him. The dark twisting of pain, hatred and power that had trailed them all into Anuin was no longer the awesome shadow of wizardry, but something they all recognized. Morgon's eyes, moving from face to face, found Deth's. He stopped; Raederle, her mind, open, vulnerable, felt the memories shock through

197

him to his core. He began to walk again, slowly; the Kings shifted without sound, away from the harpist. Deth, his head bent, seemed to be listening to the final steps of the long journey that had begun for them both at Erlenstar Mountain. When Morgon reached him, he lifted his face, the lines on it etched mercilessly in the sunlight.

He said evenly, "What strictures of justice did you take at Erlenstar Mountain out of the brain of the High One?"

Morgon's hand lifted, cracked across the harpist's face in a furious, back-handed blow that made even Farr blink. The harpist recovered his balance with an effort.

Morgon said, his voice husked with pain, "I learned enough. From both of you. I am not interested in an argument over justice. I am interested in killing you. But because we are in a King's hall, and your blood will stain his floor, it would seem courteous to explain why I am spilling it. I got tired of your harping."

"It broke the silence."

"Is there nothing in this world that will break your silence?" His words bounced shapelessly back and forth in the high corners. "I must have done enough screaming in that mountain to shatter any silence but yours. You were well-trained by the Founder. There's nothing of you I can touch. Except your life. And even that I wonder if you value."

"Yes. I value it."

"You would never beg for it. I begged for death from Ghisteslwchlohm; he ignored me. That was his mistake. But he was wise enough to run. You should have started running that day you led me into that mountain. You aren't a fool. You might have known the Star-Bearer could survive what the Prince of Hed could not. Yet you stayed and played me songs of Hed until I wept in my dreams. I could have broken your harp strings with a thought."

"You did. Several times."

"And you did not have the sense to run."

There seemed, in the absolute silence of the hall, an odd illusion of privacy about them both. The Kings, their faces battle-weary and runnelled with bitterness, looked as engrossed as if they were watching a segment of their own lives. Duac, she could tell, was still struggling with the idea of the Founder in Erlenstar Mountain; Rood had stopped struggling. His face was drained of all expression. He watched, swallowing now and then the shout or the tears gathering in his throat.

The harpist, pausing a little before he spoke, said, "No. I am a fool. Perhaps I gambled that you might pursue the master and ignore the servant. Or that even then, you might have held, as you could not hold the land-rule, something of the tenets of riddle-mastery."

Morgon's hands closed, but he kept them still. "What have the sterile tenets of an empty College to do with either my life or your death?"

"Perhaps nothing. It was a passing thought. Like my harping. An abstract question that a man with a sword at his side rarely pauses to contemplate. The implications of action."

"Words."

"Perhaps."

"You're a Master—what stricture was strong enough to keep you adhering to the tenets of riddle-mastery? The first stricture of the Founder of Lungold: the language of truth is the language of power—truth of name, truth of essence. You found the essence of betrayal more to your taste. Who are you to judge me if I find the name of revenge, murder, justice—what name you want to put to it—more to my liking?"

"Who is anyone to judge you? You are the Star-Bearer. As you hounded me across Hel, Raederle mistook you for Ghisteslwchlohm."

She saw him flinch. Rood, the breath scraping in his throat, whispered, "Morgon, I swear, tenets or no tenets, if you don't kill him, I will."

"It is, as I said, an abstract question. Rood's idea of justice makes much more sense." Deth's voice sounded dry, tired, finished.

Morgon, an agony breaking into his face, screamed at him in a voice that must have reverberated through the black caverns of Erlenstar Mountain, "What is it you want of me?" He touched the air at his side, and the great starred sword startled into shape. It lifted, blurred in his hands. Raederle knew that she would see them locked forever that way: the harpist unarmed, unmoved, his head lifting to the rise of the sword as it cut upward through the sunlight, the powerful gathering of Morgon's muscles as he swung the blade in a double-handed stroke that brought it to balance at the apex of its ascent. Then the harpist's eyes fell to Morgon's face. He whispered, "They were promised a man of peace."

The sword, hovering oddly, knotted strands of light from the windows. The harpist stood under the raw edge of its shadow with a familiar stillness that seemed suddenly, to Raederle, in its implications, more terrible than anything she had seen either in herself or in Morgon. A sound broke out of her, a protest against the glimpse of that patience, and she felt Duac's hand pull at her. But she could not move. Light shivered abruptly down the blade. The sword fell, crashed with a spattering of blue sparks against the floor. The

hilt, rebounding, came to rest with the stars face
down on the stones.

There was not a sound in the room but Morgon's breathing, shuddering uncontrollably through
him. He faced the harpist, his hands clenched at
his sides; he did not move or speak. The harpist,
gazing back at him, stirred a little. The blood
came suddenly back into his face. His lips moved
as though he were about to speak, but the word
faltered against Morgon's unrelenting silence. He
took a step backward, as in question. Then his
head bowed. He turned, his own hands closed,
walked swiftly and quietly through the motionless
Kings, out of the hall, his head, unhooded, still
bent under the weight of the sun.

Morgon stared, unseeing, at the assembly of living and dead. The unresolved, explosive turmoil
in him hung like a dangerous spell over the room.
Raederle, standing beside Rood and Duac, unable
to move in the threat of it, wondered what word
would bring Morgon's thoughts back from the
black, inescapable caverns of stone, and the blind
corner of truth into which the harpist had led him.
He seemed, recognizing none of them, a stranger,
dangerous with power; but as she waited for whatever shape that power would take, she realized
slowly that it had just shaped itself, and that he
had given them his name. She spoke it softly, almost hesitantly, knowing and not knowing the man
to whom it belonged.

"Star-Bearer."

His eyes went to her; the silence ebbed away
between his fingers as they loosened. The expression welling back into his face drew her toward
him across the hall. She heard Rood start to speak
behind her; his voice broke on a harsh, dry sob
and Duac murmured something. She stood before

the Star-Bearer, brought him with a touch out of the grip of his memories.

She whispered, "Who were promised a man of peace?"

He shuddered then, reached out to her. She put her arms around him, resting the skull on his shoulder like a warning against any interruption. "The children . . ."

She felt a tremor of awe run through her. "The Earth-Masters' children?"

"The children of stone, in that black cave . . ." His hold of her tightened. "He gave me that choice. And I thought he was defenseless. I should have—I should have remembered what deadly weapons he could forge out of words."

"Who is he? That harpist?"

"I don't know. But I do know this: I want him named." He was silent then, for a long while, his face hidden against her. He moved finally, said something she could not hear; she drew back a little. He felt the bone against his face. He reached up, took the skull. He traced an eye socket with his thumb, then looked at her. His voice, worn raw, was calmer.

"I watched you, that night on Hallard Blackdawn's lands. I was near you every night as you moved through An. No one, living or dead, would have touched you. But you never needed my help."

"I felt you near," she whispered. "But I thought —I thought you were—"

"I know."

"Well, then—well, then, what did you think I was trying to do?" Her voice rose. "Did you think I was trying to protect Deth?"

"That's exactly what you were doing."

She stared at him wordlessly, thinking of all she had done during those strange, interminable days.

She burst out, "But you still stayed with me, to protect me?" He nodded. "Morgon, I told you what I am; you could see what dark power I was waking in me—you knew its origins. You knew I am kin to those shape-changers who tried to kill you, you thought I was helping the man who had betrayed you—Why in Hel's name did you trust me?"

His hands, circling the gold crown on the skull, closed on the worn metal with sudden strength, "I don't know. Because I chose to. Then, and forever. Is that how long you intend to carry this skull around?"

She shook her head, mute again, and held out her hand for it, to give it back to Farr. The little, angular, blonde-colored pattern on her palm shone clear in the light; Morgon's hand dropped abruptly to her wrist.

"What is that?"

She resisted the impulse to close her fingers over it. "It came—it came out the first time I held fire. I used a stone from King's Mouth Plain to elude the Ymris war-ships, with an illusion of light. While I was bound to it, looking into it, I saw a man holding it, as though I were looking into a memory. I almost—I was always just on the verge of knowing him. Then I felt one of the shape-changers in my mind, wanting his name, and the bidding was broken. The stone is lost, but . . . the pattern of it burned into my hand."

His hand loosened, lay with a curious gentleness on her wrist. She looked up at him; the fear in his face chilled her heart. He put his arms around her again with the same gentleness, as if she might drift away from him like a mist and only blind hope could keep her there.

The rasp of metal on the stones made them both turn. Duac, who had picked the starred sword up off the floor, said apprehensively to Morgon, "What is it? On her hand?"

He shook his head. "I don't know. I only know that for a year Ghisteslwchlohm searched my mind for a piece of knowledge, went again and again through every moment of my life looking for one certain face, one name. That might have been it."

"Whose name?" Duac asked. Raederle, horror shooting through her, dropped her face against Morgon's shoulder.

"He never bothered to tell me."

"If they want the stone, they can find it themselves," Raederle said numbly. He had not answered Duac's question, but he would answer her, later. "No one—the shape-changer could learn nothing from me. It's in the sea with Peven's crown . . ." She lifted her head suddenly, said to Duac, "I believe our father knew. About the High One. And about—probably about me."

"I wouldn't doubt it." Then he added wearily, "I think he was born knowing everything. Except how to find his way home."

"Is he in trouble?" Morgon asked. Duac looked at him surprisedly a moment. Then he shook his head.

"I don't—I don't think so. I don't feel it."

"Then I know where he might have gone. I'll find him."

Rood crossed the hall to join them. His face was tear-stained; it held the familiar, austere expression that he carried with him into his studies and his battles. He said softly to Morgon, "I'll help you."

"Rood—"

"He's my father. You are the greatest Master in this realm. And I am an Apprentice. And may I be buried next to Farr in Hel if I watch you walk out of this hall the same way you walked into it: alone."

"He won't," Raederle said.

Duac protested, his voice lowering. "You can't leave me alone with all these Kings, Rood. I don't even know half their names. Those in this hall may have been subdued for a little while, but for how long? Aum will rise, and west Hel; there are about five people in An who might not panic, and you and I are among them."

"I am?"

"No wraith," Morgon said shortly, "will enter this house again." He weighed the skull in his hand, as they watched him, then tossed it across the room to Farr. The King caught it soundlessly, vaguely startled, as if he had forgotten whose it was. Morgon surveyed the still, ghostly assembly. He said, to them, "Do you want a war? I'll give you one. A war of desperation, for the earth itself. If you lose it, you may drift like sorrow from one end of the realm to another without finding a place to rest. What honor—if the dead are concerned with honor—can you take running Cyn Croeg's bull to death?"

"There's revenge," Farr suggested pointedly.

"Yes. There's that. But I will seal this house against you stone by stone if I must. I will do what you force me to do. And I am not concerned with honor, either." He paused, then added slowly, "Or with the bindings and unbindings of the dead of An."

"You have no such power over the dead of An," Oen said abruptly. It was a question. Something hard as the ground floor of Erlenstar Mountain surfaced in Morgon's eyes.

"I learned," he said, "from a master. You can fight your private, meaningless battles into oblivion. Or you can fight those who gave Oen his land-

heir, and who will destroy Anuin, Hel, the earth
that binds you, if you let them. And that," he
added, "should appeal to you both."

Even the Falconer asked, "How much choice
do we have?"

"I don't know. Maybe none." His hands closed
suddenly; he whispered, "I swear by my name that
if I can, I will give you a choice."

There was silence again, from the living and
the dead. Morgon turned almost reluctantly to
Duac, a question in his eyes that Duac, his instincts channelled to the heartbeat of An, understood.

He said brusquely, "Do what you want in this
land. Ask what you need from me. I'm no Master,
but I can grasp the essentials of what you have
said and done in this house. I can't begin to understand. I don't know how you could have any
power over the land-law of An. You and my father, when you find him, can argue over that later.
All I know is that there is an instinct in me to
trust you blindly. Beyond reason, and beyond
hope."

He lifted the sword in his hands, held it out to
Morgon. The stars kindled the sunlight to an unexpected beauty. Morgon, staring at Duac, did
not move. He started to speak, but no words
came. He turned suddenly toward the empty threshold; Raederle, watching him, wondered what he
was seeing beyond the courtyard, beyond the walls
of Anuin. His hand closed finally on the stars; he
took the sword from Duac.

"Thank you." They saw then in his face the
faint, troubled dawning of curiosity, and a memory that seemed to hold no pain. He lifted his other
hand, touched Raederle's face and she smiled. He
said hesitantly, "I have nothing to offer you. Not
even Peven's crown. Not even peace. But can you

bear waiting for me a little longer? I wish I knew how long. I need to go to Hed awhile, and then to Lungold. I'll try to—I'll try—"

Her smile faded. "Morgon of Hed," she said evenly, "if you take one step across that threshold without me, I will lay a curse on your next step and your next until no matter where you go your path will lead you back to me."

"Raederle—"

"I can do it. Do you want to watch me?"

He was silent, struggling between his longing and his fear for her. He said abruptly, "No. All right. Will you wait for me in Hed? I think I can get us both safely that far."

"No."

"Then will you—"

"No."

"All right; then—"

"No."

"Then will you come with me?" he whispered. "Because I could not bear to leave you."

She put her arms around him, wondering, as she did so, what strange, perilous future she had bargained for. She said only, as his arms circled her, not in gentleness this time, but in a fierce and terrified determination, "That's good. Because I swear by Ylon's name you never will."

———

HEIR OF SEA AND FIRE *is the second of three*

books about Morgon, Raederle, the world they

live in and the end of an age.

THE RIDDLE-MASTER OF HED *is the first.*

People and Places

ACOR OF HEL   third King of Hel

ALOIL   a Lungold wizard

AN   Kingdom incorporating the Three Portions
(An, Aum, Hel); ruled by Mathom

ANUIN   seaport in An; home of the Kings of An

ASTRIN   Ymris land-heir; brother of Heureu

AUM   ancient kingdom conquered by An; under
Mathom's rule

BERE   Dana Isig's grandson

BLACKDAWN, HALLARD—a lord of An, with lands
in east Hel

CAERWEDDIN   city in Ymris, home of the Kings of
Ymris, on the mouth of the Thul River

CAITHNARD   seaport and traders' city; site of the
College of Riddle-Masters

CORBETT, BRI   ship-master of Mathom of An

CORRIG   a shape-changer; Ylon's father

CROEG, CYN   the Lord of Aum, with lands in east Aum; a descendant of the Kings of Aum

CROEG, MARA   Cyn Croeg's wife; The Flower of An

CYONE   Mathom's wife; mother of Duac, Rood and Raederle

DANAN ISIG   land-ruler, King of Isig

DETH   a harpist

DUAC   Mathom's son; land-heir of An

EARTH-MASTERS   ancient, mysterious inhabitants of the High One's realm

EL   Elrhiarhodan, the land-ruler of Herun

ELIARD   the Prince of Hed; Morgon's younger brother

ELIEU OF HEL   the younger brother of Raith, Lord of Hel

ERIEL   a shape-changer; a kinswoman of Corrig and Raederle

ERLENSTAR MOUNTAIN   ancient home of the High One

EVERN   "The Falconer"; a dead King of Hel

FARR   the last of the Kings of Hel

GHISTESLWCHLOHM   Founder of the School of Wizards at Lungold

HAR   the Wolf-King; land-ruler of Osterland

HARTE   mountain-home of Danan Isig

HED   tiny island ruled by the Princes of Hed

HEL   one of the Three Portions of An, conquered by the Kings of An

HERUN   a small kingdom ruled by the Morgols of Herun

HEUREU   the King of Ymris

HIGH ONE   an Earth-Master; sustainer of the land-law of his realm

HLURLE   a small trade-port near Herun

HWILLION, MAP   a young lord with lands in south Aum

IFF   a Lungold wizard

IMER   a guard in the Morgol's service

ISIG   a mountain-kingdom, ruled by Danan Isig

ISIG PASS   a mountain pass between Isig and Erlenstar Mountain

KIA   a guard in the Morgol's service

KING'S MOUTH PLAIN   site of one of the Earth-Master's ruined cities, north of Caerweddin

KRAAL   port-city at the mouth of the Winter River, in Osterland

KYRTH   trade-city in Isig, on the Ose River

LUNGOLD   city founded by Ghisteslwchlohm; home of the School of Wizards

LYRA   the land-heir of Herun; El's daughter

MADIR   ancient witch of An

MASTER, CANNON   a farmer of Hed

MATHOM   King of An

MORGON   the Star-Bearer

NEMIR   Nemir of the Pigs; a dead King of Hel

NUN   A Lungold Wizard

OEN OF AN   King of An, father of Ylon

OHROE OF HEL   a dead King of Hel; called "The Cursed"

OSTERLAND   northern Kingdom, ruled by Har

RAEDERLE   daughter of Cyone and Mathom of An

RAITH   the Lord of Hel, descendant of the ancient Kings of Hel

ROOD   Mathom's younger son

TEL   a Master at the College at Caithnard

TRIKA   a guard in the Morgol's service

TRISTAN   Morgon's sister

YLON   an ancient King of An; son of Oen of An
   and the shape-changer Corrig

YMIRIS   a Kingdom, ruled by Heureu Ymris

PATRICIA A. MCKILLIP discovered the joys of writing when she was fourteen, endured her teen-age years in the secret life of her stories, plays and novels, and has been writing ever since—except for a brief detour when she thought she would be a concert pianist.

She was born in Salem, Oregon and has lived in Arizona, California and the England that is the setting for *The House on Parchment Street*. After a number of years in San Jose, where she received an MA in English from San Jose State University, she moved to San Francisco, where she now lives.

Miss McKillip has also written *The Throme of the Erril of Sherill*, *The Forgotten Beasts of Eld*, *The Night Gift*, and *The Riddle-Master of Hed*.

TOLKIEN

HUMPHREY CARPENTER

Now, Tolkien's life is recreated through diaries, private papers, letters and living memory, in a vivid portrait of the man who invented a whole magical world beloved by millions. This authorized account illuminates his epic work and provides a wonderful introduction for those who have never met the hobbits, wizards, dragons, elves and orcs who populate Middle-earth.

BB

Ballantine Books
27256/$2.50

LG-6

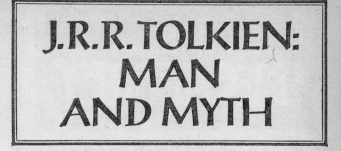

J.R.R.TOLKIEN: MAN AND MYTH

___TOLKIEN: A BIOGRAPHY,
Humphrey Carpenter   27256   2.50
The authorized biography of the man who cre-
ated Middle-earth. "A treasure!"—*Chicago Tribune
Book World.* "Succeeds remarkably."—*Newsweek.*
A Book-of-the-Month Club Alternate Selection.

___TOLKIEN: A Look Behind *The Lord of the Rings,*
Lin Carter   27539   1.95
A joyous exploration of Tolkien's classic trilogy.
Relates this modern masterpiece to the long his-
tory of magnificent epics of which it is both a part
and a glorious example.

___A GUIDE TO MIDDLE EARTH,
Robert Foster   27547   2.25
A definitive concordance for Tolkien's masterful
trilogy, *The Lord of the Rings,* with a glossary of
people, places, and things—arranged for conven-
ient reference.

___MASTER OF MIDDLE EARTH,
Paul H. Kocher   27850   2.25
An entertaining and perceptive study of Tolkien's
fiction. "A winner...impels the reader to return and
reread Tolkien with new insight."—*Library Journal*

___J. R. R. TOLKIEN:
MAN AND MYTH BOXED SET   27910   8.95
Includes TOLKIEN: A BIOGRAPHY, TOLKIEN: A
LOOK BEHIND *THE LORD OF THE RINGS,* A GUIDE
TO MIDDLE EARTH, and MASTER OF MIDDLE
EARTH.

🅑🅑 Ballantine Books   LG-7